CONTENTS

1.	ELISABETH	1
2.	TIM	8
3.	VERONICA	15
4.	FELIX	18
5.	MOLLY	23
6.	FELIX	31
7.	MOLLY	36
8.	TIM	39
9.	MOLLY	45
10.	VERONICA	50
11.	MOLLY	52
12.	VERONICA	55
13.	VERONICA	61
14.	MOLLY	69
15.	FRANK	73
16.	VERONICA	76
17.	MOLLY	83
18.	VERONICA	89

19.	MOLLY	95
20.	VERONICA	99
21.	MOLLY	102
22.	VERONICA	106
23.	TIM	108
24.	VERONICA	112
25.	VERONICA	116
26.	TIM	120
27.	VERONICA	123
28.	VERONICA	126
29.	TIM	133
30.	VERONICA	140
31.	VERONICA	149
32.	HELENA	152
33.	VERONICA	161
34.	HELENA	166
35.	VERONICA	171
36.	HELENA	176
37.	VERONICA	180
38.	HELENA	182
39.	VERONICA	187
40.	HELENA	194
41.	TIM	196
42.	VERONICA	200

43. HELENA 204

1

ELISABETH

"Felicia, darling?"

The young woman turns around at the sound of Elisabeth's voice. She's carrying a bunch of white linen.

"Are those the sheets from Alan's bed?"

"Yes. I thought I would change them."

"Thank you, but ... you're making a mess."

Elisabeth points at the tile floor. There's a trail of gray stuff.

"Oh. I'm very sorry. I will vacuum the floor."

"Make sure you do," Elisabeth tells her, then turns around and—

—hears a sound and abruptly sits up in the chair. She looks around and finds herself in the hallway of the detention facility. The cops are sitting down too, closer to the door. One of them is looking at his phone, the other fiddling with his weapon. None of them seem to have noticed Elisabeth drifted off.

She was back in time. Her mind her replayed the last time she saw Felicia. She wishes she'd been a little more friendly towards the maid.

Discreetly, she adjusts her hair and sits up a little straighter. An awful headache starts throbbing at the back of her skull. Lack of sleep, too much worry. On her lap sits Prince. The dog stirs and looks up at her.

"It's okay, honey," she mutters, clearing her throat. "Go back to sleep."

The dog glances over at the door, as though longing to see Alan.

Elisabeth longs to see him too. She knows logically it won't happen. Lundbeck explained to her how this isn't a regular disease and that it's extremely unlikely a cure will come around.

Yet she can't help but hope despite everything.

Alan is her life, her rock. Before they met, Lis was a wreck. She'd gone through three volatile marriages in just ten years, all of her husbands abusive, both physically and emotionally. She never thought she would meet someone like Alan. He can be harsh, sure, but he's never raised his hand against her, and he always makes her feel safe.

They argue now and then, as all married couples do, but it's almost always Lis's own insecurities that bring it about—her jealousy, her need for control, her lack of trust in him—but unlike her previous husbands, Alan is never provoked by her unfounded accusations or her unreasonable demands. Which is why things never escalate between them.

Basically, they're a great match, and Lis loves him with all her heart. Meeting Alan even made her want to try and have kids. Unfortunately, Lis turned out to be infertile due to uterine polyps. So they got Prince instead. Eleven years old, he's still their baby.

She bends over and plants a kiss on the dog's head. He looks up at her and wags his tail.

"Daddy will be all right," she tells him. "I'm sure of it. Let's pray again."

She folds her hands, closes her eyes, and asks God for the umpteenth time to please bring Alan back to her.

Just as she whispers "Amen," the noise comes again. The one that woke her up.

It's a weird, dry sound. Almost like old wood breaking. Prince hears it too, and he looks over at the door again. The guards don't seem to notice it, despite the fact that they're closer to the cell.

Come to think of it, Alan has been very quiet for the last hour or so. The tranquilizer they shot him with lasts about forty-five minutes.

"Excuse me?"

The guards don't hear her.

"Excuse me?"

The one closest to her looks over at her. His expression is tired. It's no wonder; he's been up all night, too. "Yeah?"

"Isn't it time for another shot?"

The guard checks his watch. "Yeah, guess you're right. But he's not saying anything, so ..."

The guard goes back to doing whatever it is he's doing with his gun without even bothering to get up and check on Alan.

"But I just heard him make a noise," Lis persists.

"I didn't hear anything," the guard says, not looking at her.

Elisabeth huffs and gets to her feet. Setting Prince down on the chair, she goes to the door and looks through the window.

At first, she can't see Alan anywhere, and she almost panics. He's not on the bed, where he spends most of the time. Not on the floor, either. Lis stands on her toes to look down and make sure he's not lying up against the door, either. He's not.

Then she notices the chains. They replaced the bedpost that Alan tore free when Tim was here, and now he's got a chain around both ankles. The chains are still fixed to the bed. But strangely, from there, they run upwards.

Lis follows them with her eyes. It takes her several seconds to realize what the thing sitting in the corner below the ceiling is. It looks like a sleeping bag. Except it's not made of fabric but some sort of organic material. And it's transparent in places. Through the strange membrane, she can see Alan. He's curled up into a fetal position, and he's hanging upside down.

"What the heck?" Lis breathes.

Her voice makes the guard finally get to his feet. "What's wrong?"

"I don't … I don't know," she says, prying her eyes off of Alan to let the guard see.

Just like it did for Lis, it takes the guard a few seconds to locate Alan. When he does, he frowns. "Shit. Well, that's new."

"What?" the other guard says, joining them.

"He's spun himself into a pupa," the first guard grunts. "Like a fucking larva."

"That's my husband you're talking about!" Lis hears herself snap.

The guards ignore her. Prince whimpers from the chair.

"Damn," the other guard says. "We'd better call Lundbeck."

"Think she's back?"

"I don't know." The guard takes out his phone and makes a call.

Lis steps closer and looks in at Alan again. The guard is right; the thing wrapped around Alan does look an awful lot like a cocoon. "Alan? Darling, can you still hear me?"

No answer. She can make out one of Alan's eyes through the membrane. It's closed, as though he's sleeping. It looks like he's surrounded by some kind of thick liquid. Eyeing it closely, Lis can tell the cocoon—or whatever it is—is slightly pulsating slowly. Like a giant lung breathing. The transparency of the cocoon fades along with the pulse. She stares at Alan's hand. All six fingers are visible when the membrane is the most see-through. And she can tell the fingers are a lot shorter than they used to be. The tips seem to fade. With each pulsation, Lis gets another glimpse of Alan's hand. And she can tell the fingers are growing noticeably shorter.

They're dissolving. He's dissolving.

The thought is so horrifying, she can't say it out loud. She staggers back, clasping a hand over her mouth.

"What is it?"

A familiar voice makes her turn her head. Lundbeck comes striding down the corridor.

"You tell us, boss," one of the guards says, gesturing at the cell door. "You heard of anything like this?"

Lundbeck stops by the door and looks into the cell. When she sees Alan, she exhales. "Oh, fuck me ... that can't be good."

"Is he dead?" the other guard asks.

"Looks pretty alive to me," the other remarks.

"You need to help him," Lis hears her own voice say. "You need to do something. Before he's ... before he's turned completely into ..." She breaks into tears.

"Get her to the breakroom," Lundbeck tells one of the guards. "You shouldn't see this, Lis."

"Oh, God ... oh, please, God ..."

The guard takes her by the arm, and Prince snaps his teeth at him.

"Damnit. Get that dog under control, will you?"

Lis is about to answer, when the sound comes again. The sound of dry wood breaking. It's much louder this time, and it clearly comes from Alan's cell.

All of them look at the door. From her position, Elisabeth can just make out the corner of the cocoon. As she stares at it, it suddenly turns hard. It happens within seconds. Like water freezing over at record speed. The transparency goes, and Alan disappears. The noise comes again. Then the cocoon stars shaking. It's a subtle vibration at first, but then it begins trembling violently. It could be her imagination, but Lis is certain she can feel the tremors in the floor.

"Jesus Christ," Lundbeck breathes, backing away from the door. She whips her head around and stares at the guards. "Get everyone out of here. Right now. I think he's about to—"

Lundbeck never gets to finish the sentence. The door to the cell comes crashing out, smashing the nearest guard into the wall. Something black and cloudlike bursts out into the hallway, knocking them all off their feet. There's a sound too, a loud bang, like a gigantic balloon popping. It slams against Lis's eardrums, turning her deaf on the spot.

She scrambles to get back up. She can't see anything; the black stuff is everywhere. She breathes it in with a raspy gasp, feels it fill her lungs. It's in her nose, her ears, her eyes. Crawling, she calls out for Prince, not hearing her own voice. She feels like she's about to suffocate, when suddenly, the black stuff eases off a little. Looking around, Lis can actually see now. It's like she's inside a heavy fog, but she can make out the hallway, the chairs, Lundbeck, the guards, the torn-off door. And Prince. He gets to his feet, sneezes and shakes his fur. Then he runs to Lis and she picks him up and she gets to her feet.

Lundbeck and one of the guards are getting up too. Lis doesn't wait around. She makes her way down the hallway to the back door. It's already open—or rather, it's gone. Apparently, the shockwave was strong enough to burst this door open, too.

Lis staggers outside, coughing and wiping at her eyes to get the black stuff off. She walks away from the building, hoping to get out of range of the black fog, and it does get a little less thick, but surprisingly, it's still in the air, even out here.

Finally, she turns around and looks back at the facility. And it dawns on her just how powerful the explosion was. Every single window has been blown open, and the black stuff is oozing out of the building like smoke from a fire. It doesn't rise to the sky, though. It spreads out sideways, expanding in concentric waves, swallowing up the nearby houses.

Lis realizes her hearing is returning. She can hear Prince whimper and cough. She can hear people screaming. And she can hear her own heartbeat, hammering away in her chest.

2

TIM

TIM DOESN'T UNDERSTAND WHAT he's seeing.

Helena is dead. He knows that for sure. He felt her bleed out.

And yet he's looking into her eyes, and she's clearly looking back at him. She blinks slowly, as though waking from a pleasant sleep, and a smile creases the corners of her eyes.

"Hey, Dad," she says softly.

"Hey," he croaks back, thinking to himself, *Are we both dead? Or did I just lose my mind?*

"Are you ... okay?" she asks.

Tim nods, feeling like he's caught up in a dream. "Yeah, I'm fine. How are *you* feeling?"

"Tired," she admits. "And a little cold. But other than that ..." She shrugs and smiles again.

It's only now Tim becomes aware his palm is still pressed against Helena's neck. It's sticky with blood. He's afraid to take it away. Afraid that his hand has somehow provided a temporary Band-Aid that's keeping his daughter artificially alive. But the rational part of his brain knows that can't be the case. And besides, the blood is no longer flowing. Which can only mean Helena's veins are empty, and her heart has ceased beating.

Except it hasn't.

He can feel her pulse, slow but strong.

"What ... what's happening?" he asks.

Helena blinks. "I don't know. I thought I was dying."

Tim finally musters the courage to ease off just enough that his palm loses contact with her neck. It lets go with a soft, sticky sound. Tim stares at the blood-smeared skin of his daughter's neck. He expects to see the gash. To see fresh blood come spilling out.

But he sees neither.

In the middle of all the half-dried blood, he sees the wound all right. Except something strange has happened to it. Somehow, time seems to have been fast-forwarded several days. Because the wound is closed and well on its way to healing completely.

Tim blinks several times, a feeling of unreality flooding over him.

"What is it, Dad?" Helena asks, searching his face. "What happened to me?"

"You're all right," he hears himself say. "I think ... I think God healed you."

Helena raises her hand and lets her fingertips run over the wound. She looks at them. Then she takes Tim's hand and looks at his palm. And finally, her eyes meet his. "No, Dad. I think *you* healed me."

She turns over his hand, and Tim stares at his own palm. At first, he can only see Helena's blood. But then he notices something odd. Right in the middle of his palm is an almond shaped area, the exact size of Helena's wound, where the skin is slightly raised. It's wrinkled and mushy, like when you've been soaking in a bath for an hour.

"Holy ... shit," Tim mutters, as it finally hits home. He looks at Helena, and an awkward smile tugs at the corner of his mouth. "I didn't ... I didn't know I could do that."

Helena smiles, and her eyes fill up with tears. "I love you, Dad." She raises her arms to embrace him, and Tim scoops her up into a tight hug.

"I love you, too, sweetheart. More than anything in this world."

It's probably the best moment of Tim's life. Better than when Helena was born. And it lasts for all of ten seconds, before he hears a sound and turns his head.

The door has been opened, and the fat woman is standing there, staring at her phone, which is in turn aimed at Tim and Helena. Her eyes are wide, her mouth open in disbelief.

"You've gotta be fucking kidding me," Tim growls, letting go of Helena as he gets to his feet. Standing at what's got to be close to nine feet now, the sight of Tim is enough to cause the woman to draw back a little. It pleases him to see fear on her face—serves her right for blatantly prying on such a private moment. "What the hell are you looking at?"

The woman mutters something, finally stops recording, turns around and lumbers off.

"Dad ... are you ... are you hurt?"

Tim looks down and sees that Helena has gotten to her feet. She gently touches his side where the woman got him. He can already feel the wounds closing.

"I'm fine," he says automatically. His strength suddenly fails him. It's only now he feels just how exhausted he is.

Helena grabs him, as though she could stop him from falling. "Are you sure you're OK, Dad?"

"I'm just a little worn," he mutters, leaning on the table. "It's been a long day. It'll be fine."

He smiles at her, then sighs from relief and exhaustion. His legs are trembling, so he pulls out a chair and sits down.

"So, what happens now?" Helena asks, glancing towards the door.

Tim rubs his face. "They've got a lot of cleaning up to do. But they're on it. I'm sure they'll get it done."

Downstairs, Tim can hear policemen flooding into the building. Judging by the sounds from outside, they have closed down the entire street and are evacuating the building.

"What about you, Dad?" Helena sits down next to him, searching his face.

He shrugs. "They'll need to do some prodding and probing if they're to find a cure for this, and I'm the only subject that won't fight them."

She's looking at him intently now. "So you'll be locked up?"

"Yeah, I guess so."

"And you won't come out again, will you? Like, ever?"

He looks back at her, hating that she has to see him like this—a badly beaten-up freak. Amazingly, she doesn't seem too bothered about it, though. "Probably not, no. I don't think it's likely they'll reverse this."

Helena tears up but bites her lip to keep it back.

Then, surprising him, she says, "Let's go, Dad."

At first, he thinks she means for them to go meet the cops and let them take him away. But her eyes are suddenly fierce.

"Go where?" he asks.

"Go wherever they won't bother you."

He grunts. "That's a wonderful idea. But I gave them my word, honey."

Helena gives that groan of exasperation he's heard her utter so many times in the past whenever they clashed or she came up against his stupid, stubborn principles. She knows what his word means. She knows he won't break a promise, even for her.

"Listen, sweetie," he tells her. "I'll make sure we get to see each other. But this is too important. If I can help them in any way, I have to do it. Even if there's only the slightest chance. After all, I started all this mess, so it's my ..." He trails off as Helena's attention is caught by something else. She takes out her phone, reads a text, then frowns.

"Oh, Jeez," she whispers. "Dennis just texted me. Look, Dad ..."

She turns over the phone. It's a news video that shows shaky overhead images from a city somewhere. It appears to be from last night, because everything is grey and murky, as though the sun hasn't risen yet. But the caption at the bottom reads, LIVE FROM HORNSTED: TOXIC OUTBREAK OF UNKNOWN INFECTANT.

The camera hones in on a building he recognizes: the detention facility where they keep Alan. It looks like an anthill that someone has disturbed. People are running around, clearly distressed about something. He can't see any dangers at first. Not until they zoom in to show the black stuff. And he finally realizes why the scene is so murky.

The black stuff not only covers everything within sight: cars, pavement, the building ... it's also littering the air like ashes from a huge fire. The people on the screen are smothered in it. The camera zooms out to show the extent of it. It has reached several blocks down. Covering a circle over three hundred yards across with the detention facility at the center.

"Fuckin' hell," Tim mutters. "What happened ...?"

He can hear cops downstairs now, shouting to each other, making their way through the building.

"This is ... this is bad, right?" Helena asks.

"I don't know," he lies, and pulls out the phone. He calls up Lundbeck, not really expecting an answer.

She picks up almost right away. "*Yeah?*" Her voice is strained, and she breaks off into a coughing fit.

"Jesus Christ, what happened, Ulla?"

Lundbeck finishes coughing, spits and snorts. "*He exploded, Tim. He fucking blew up.*"

Tim feels his gut sink and the floor turn soft under his feet. "You back there already?"

"*Yeah, we flew right back the minute we dropped you off ... wish I hadn't, but ...*" She coughs again.

"How ... how bad is it?" Tim croaks. He's aware of Helena staring at him.

"*Bad,*" Lundbeck tells him. "*Irreparable, probably. We've got at least a hundred infected people on the loose now. Every single one of my men on the scene got a lethal dose. Even those of us wearing masks. It just ... it just forced its way in. And it's everywhere, Tim. Remember how we worried if it was airborne ...?*" She laughs hoarsely, then coughs some more. "*Oh, it's airborne, all right. It's blown across half the fucking town by now.*"

"Oh, no," Tim mutters, realizing at last the full scope of things. "It can't be stopped."

"*Nope, that's my guess, too. We're gonna keep working, but ... within half an hour, we'll all be ... well ...*"

She doesn't need to finish the sentence.

"Fuck. I'm ... I'm really sorry, Ulla. I feel responsible for this."

Then Lundbeck says something Tim really didn't expect. "*If not you, then someone else.*" She states it very matter-of-factly. And it's probably true. This was always inevitable. This thing had come here to win, and it would have found a way even if Tim had never gone out there to check out the boulder. It still doesn't do much to ease his conscience, though.

"*I'm gonna call my daughter now, Tim.*" Another brief coughing fit. "*I suggest you find your loved ones too. Take good care of them.*" Then she simply hangs up.

Tim slips the phone back into his pocket. Helena is still staring at him. She probably heard it all.

"Is this it?" she asks. "Is this how the world ends, Dad?"

Tim breathes a couple of times. "Certainly looks that way, yeah."

"Are you still ... are you still turning yourself in?"

He shakes his head. "Wouldn't do any good now."

"Oh, thank God!"

Her expression of relief is so sincere and so misplaced, it almost makes Tim laugh. They just found out that mankind is expiring rapidly, and still, what matters more to her is that he won't leave her side.

Humans are funny.

"So where are we going, Dad?"

He replays in his mind what Lundbeck said just before she disconnected. She was right. This was no longer about saving the world. That ship sailed when Alan exploded. Now, it's about keeping your loved ones alive. And Tim has one more living family member to take care of. A four-legged one. He gets to his feet. "We're going home, honey."

3

VERONICA

Driving back proves a lot harder because of the darkness which is really thick by now.

And yet Veronica steps on it as much as she dares. The thought of Molly compels her. The snow scooter has a strong headlight, but it only reaches so far ahead, and her field of vision is limited. Obstacles will suddenly appear in front of her, and more than once she has to hit the brakes.

She tries to follow her own tracks. She can't drive directly on them, because that makes the scooter go wobbly, but she can drive right next to them, and it gives her something to follow.

Leo clearly went this way too; every hundred yards or so, his prints will cross over the tracks from the scooter. If Veronica didn't know any better, she would have thought it was prints from a deer or something, because there are several yards between each one. As though Leo is jumping more than running.

To begin with, she fears that she'll suddenly see Leo. She imagines him appearing in the light, just standing there, staring at her. Or maybe he's lurking out in the darkness, lying in wait, ready to jump her from the side, knock her off the scooter and eat her alive just like he did with the poor old couple.

But for some reason, the logical part of her brain knows that won't happen. That if Leo wanted to eat her, he would have done so at the Thomsens' house.

He definitely saw her.

He recognized her, too.

And yet he didn't come for her.

Why?

The only two answers she can think of is that either Leo was completely full from the pounds of flesh and entrails he took off the old guy. Or—and this is the explanation she's hoping for—Leo is still enough human to spare the ones he loved.

If that's the case, then there's a chance he's not headed back for the cabin to kill his family and Molly.

Although, judging by how fast he's going, he most definitely has a purpose. Even though Veronica is going upwards of twenty-five miles per hour most of the time, she doesn't catch up with Leo.

She passes the fence with the cows, and something makes her stop briefly. She lets the engine idle and pulls out the flashlight. Pointing it at the barn, she sees the cow heads protruding from the opening, gazing at her with curiosity. She sees the infected cow right away. And she can tell the black stuff is dying; it's all grey and has mostly drizzled off already. The cow hasn't transformed in any way. It doesn't even look sick.

"Good girl," Veronica mutters, shutting off the flashlight. "You kicked it."

She continues driving, and her mind wanders. She ponders about Flemming, Alice and Sylvia. Have they started to change? Or did they beat the infection? What even decided who would turn and who wouldn't? What made Veronica and Leo stand apart? What caused her to turn out fine, while Leo succumbed to the illness? It seems doubly peculiar when considering Veronica is already sick from cancer. Her system must be compromised. Weakened. Leo, on the other hand, was fit and healthy. Why hadn't she been much more vulnerable to—

It strikes her out of nowhere.

She can't know for certain whether it's true or not, but it *feels* like it's the right explanation.

*It didn't take me over **because** of the cancer. It couldn't use me because I'm already sick.*

If this explanation is true, then Sylvia should kick the infection too. Whereas Flemming and Alice will most likely turn just like Leo.

Which means that Molly by now could be holed up in the cabin with not one but two soon-to-be cannibalistic monsters. Not to mention the third one headed their way.

Veronica ups the speed even further.

4

FELIX

IT SEEMS TO TAKE them forever to get the last folks onto the bus.

Felix just lies there on the freezing pavement, shivering.

He worries what will happen once the bus drives off. He'll be completely exposed. He considers grabbing onto the underside of the bus and letting it transport him away from the airport completely unseen. But for one thing, there are no good places to hold onto, and for another, he suspects that only really works in the movies. He's not Bruce Willis. He can't be expected to hold his own body weight for several miles. His arms will probably give out sooner rather than later, causing him to flop onto the ground while the bus is still moving and hurt himself badly.

So, it's probably better to stay and chance it.

Finally, the last person from the plane steps onto the bus. The doors close, and the guards exchange a few words—Felix can't really hear what they're saying over the bus's engine.

Then, suddenly, the bus starts moving. It drives straight ahead for a few yards, and Felix makes himself as flat as he can—even though there's almost a full foot of air between him and the undercarriage. Just as the rear end gets close to Felix, the bus starts turning, and for an awful moment, he and the left tire are on a perfect collision course. Felix rolls over twice, grazing the underside of the bus with his shoulder, then lies back down on his back. A split second later, the tires pass on each side of him, and he's suddenly staring up into the gray sky.

Quickly, Felix jumps to his feet. He glances around apprehensively. There are still quite a few people around, but to his surprise and relief, no one seems to be looking at him.

Still, he feels like a deer in the headlights just standing there in the middle of the scene. Someone could turn and notice him any second, and he's sure they'll look right through his feeble disguise.

What are you doing? Move! Get out of here!

He finally gets his frozen legs going. He wants to run, to sprint for the exit, but he forces himself to walk normally, trying his best to look casual. He heads for a stair truck that's parked fifty yards off. Its engine is off, and there's no driver. A group of soldiers are headed for a truck. Others are standing in a group, talking. Felix walks right past them, keeping his gaze down.

A gruff voice shouts out from behind him: "Hey, what are you doing?"

He stops as though struck by lightning. It feels like it takes him a full minute to turn around, but it's probably only a second. He expects to see someone coming for him, maybe even a weapon pointed at him, and he instinctively holds up his hands.

But no one's coming for him. No one's even looking at him. Instead, the group of soldiers are looking at another guy. He's wearing a hazmat suit identical to the one Felix has on, and the guy has taken off the mask and pulled down the zipper.

"Get that suit back on!" the gruff-voiced soldier yells, pointing at him. "Are you trying to get yourself infected? You need to go to decontamination before you take it off."

"Right, sorry," the guy mumbles, fumbling to get the suit back on.

Felix manages to turn back around and keep walking.

Another suit-clad soldier—a female, judging by her eyes—passes him by just then, and she says something to him. Felix can't hear it, because a plane has been approaching and is now almost overhead.

"Huh?" he asks.

The woman points to a truck. "Decontamination," she repeats. "It's that way. Didn't you hear the instructions?"

"Oh. Sure. I was just ... thank you."

She rolls her eyes, then walks on. Felix waits to check if she looks back. She doesn't. So, instead of going to the truck, he continues in the direction he was headed. Reaching the stair truck, he runs around to the other side of it, and immediately begins ripping off his suit. He drops it on the ground and is about to take off running, when he sees a guy leaning against the truck door, smoking a cigarette, staring at him.

"Uhm ..." Felix mutters, dumbfounded.

The guy frowns. "Shouldn't you go with the others?"

"Yeah, no, I'm ... off duty," he says, forcing a smile.

The guy obviously doesn't buy it. For one thing, Felix is a terrible liar. For another, he's clearly not a soldier. The driver drops his cigarette, steps on it, then goes around the truck and calls out, "Hey! You guys! I think you better come over here!"

Felix's heart explodes in his chest. He looks out over the tarmac. Whichever direction he chooses, there's at least half a mile before he can reach the fence—the soldiers will catch up with him long before that.

Instead, he has an idea, and he acts upon it before he has time to second-guess it. He rips open the truck door and climbs in. The key is in the ignition. He turns it, and the stair truck comes to life instantly. He puts it in drive and takes off with a burst.

The driver, who was headed for the soldiers, still calling to them, turns around and starts yelling at Felix instead. Felix ignores him and drives off. His dad taught him how to drive last summer, and Felix is grateful for it—it just might save his life. There are no obstacles on the tarmac, so there's no real risk of him running into anything, and he guns it across the pavement.

Checking the mirrors, he sees the soldiers already so far away they look like ants. But he can tell they've caught on to the situation, and two vehicles are headed this way.

Felix reaches the fence, and he immediately realizes there is no way he is getting over it on foot—it's almost twelve feet tall and has spikes at the top, clearly meant to keep out anyone trying to enter the tarmac. On the other side is a patch of trees, and behind them is the city. If he can just make it over and disappear from sight, he can actually get away.

He parks the stair truck as close to the fence as he can, then jumps out. Running up the steps, he glances back and sees the military vehicles approaching. He hesitates only briefly before he leaps over the fence. Flying through the air, he lands on the frozen ground and rolls around several times to take the edge off the impact. Still, both his feet hurt, but he doesn't have time to worry about it. He jumps up and runs into the trees. Ignoring the branches and fir needles scratching his hands and face, he comes out on the other side, staring across a highway into the busy city.

From behind him, the soldiers are shouting.

Felix presses on, crossing the road as soon as there's a gap in the traffic, and runs down the nearest street.

He keeps running until he's several blocks over. Stopping, he heaves for breath and looks back. No one's coming.

I made it. I got away.

5

MOLLY

SHE KEEPS USING THE camera on her phone to check her eyes. Her ears. Her mouth.

Those seem to be the places the nasty black stuff appears first. At least it did so on Mom and Grandpa.

She also studies her hands every five minutes or so, particularly the palms. That's where Veronica said it came on first for her.

So far, she can't see anything.

Which is great news. And it should make her relieved. But all she feels is agitation and tenseness. She's worried about Mom and Grandpa. She's going stir-crazy. She's tried to pass the time by watching Netflix on her phone or reading the book she brought along. But she can't really focus for more than a few minutes at a time.

She looks at the window, even though she's pulled the blinds. It's dark outside now. Having been in her room all day, she really wants to get out. But Mom forbade it; she even locked the door from the outside. When Molly had to pee, she called her and asked to go to the bathroom. But Mom just brought her a bowl and a roll of toilet paper and locked the door again.

Reluctantly, Molly peed in the bowl and emptied it out the window. She found it disgusting, but what could she do?

Even though it's annoying, she understands why Mom is being so careful.

They've talked on the phone several times during the day. It's been almost an hour, so Molly decides to call her again.

This time, Mom doesn't pick up right away. In fact, she doesn't pick up at all. Not until Molly calls her up a second time.

"*Hello?*" she croaks. "*Dad?*"

"No, Mom. It's me."

"*Who?*"

"Me, Molly."

"*Oh. Hi, sweetie.*"

Baffled, Molly asks, "Didn't you recognize my voice, Mom?"

"*No, no, I did. It's just ... I was sleeping, that's all.*"

Molly imagines it probably also has something to do with the black stuff growing in Mom's ears. "Sorry to wake you up, Mom."

"*No, it's fine, I ... I need to take another aspirin anyway. I think the fever's back ...*" Mom is muttering to herself as Molly can hear her rummage around for something. "*Where's that bottle ...?*"

"How are you feeling, Mom?"

"*Huh? I'm good. I'm fine. Better, I think.*"

That's a lie if ever Molly heard one. Mom doesn't just sound like she just woke up; she sounds like she's very sick and confused. There's also something about her voice that's different. It's muffled. As though there's a cloth in front of the phone.

As though Molly's thoughts brought it about, Mom begins coughing. The sound is thick and rattly. It's loud enough that Molly can hear it from down the hallway, too.

Mom hawks and spits. Whatever comes up land somewhere close by with a wet splat. "*Oh, Jeez,*" Mom groans.

"Mom, are you sure you're all right?" Molly asks, feeling like crying. "You want me to come in there? I could bring you some—"

"*No!*" Mom barks. Then, a little calmer: "*No, stay where you are, sweetie. I'll manage.*" Mom's voice is a bit more normal now, after whatever it was has been cleared from her airways. Molly can't help but picture a big, soggy lump of the black stuff drenched with saliva, and she feels nauseous.

"Did you talk with the doctors again? Are they even coming?"

"*Yes,*" Mom says, sounding sleepy again. "*Yes, Grandpa told me they called him, and ... and they're finally coming.*"

"When?"

"*I don't know, sweetie. Look, I think I'll try and get some more ... some more sleep, okay?*"

"Okay, Mom," Molly says, really straining not to cry now. She wants to keep talking to Mom, wants to keep her awake. But at the same time, she knows sleep is good for you when you're ill. "Sleep tight."

Mom grumbles something Molly can't make out, and five seconds later she begins snoring loudly.

Molly listens for a few more minutes, not wanting to hang up. It's kind of reassuring listening to Mom sleeping.

The thought of Grandpa is what makes her disconnect the call. The last time they spoke was maybe three hours ago, when he brought her a plate of food. Just like Mom had done with the bowl, he opened the door just enough to push the plate inside. Molly noticed he was wearing a rubber glove, and she got a glimpse of his face, too. Even though Grandpa tried to smile reassuringly at her, Molly couldn't help but gasp. Grandpa didn't look like himself. The black stuff was everywhere. As soon as he closed the door, he started coughing violently. Molly heard him stagger back down the hallway.

She calls him up.

But he doesn't answer. Not on the first, second or third try.

Molly can hear his phone ringing through the door.

Finally, she gives up.

He's probably sleeping too.

At least she hopes so.

But a deeper part of her knows that's not the case. She's trying hard to tell herself that Mom and Grandpa will both be fine, that they'll beat the infection and recover fully, just like Veronica did. But she can't keep fooling herself. Veronica said she barely got sick from the strange disease before it left her again. Leo, on the other hand, fell very ill with fever and everything. Just like Mom and Grandpa.

They'll both end up like Leo—whatever happened to him.

The thought makes her cry. She can't keep in the tears any longer, so she slumps down on the bed and weeps into her pillow.

Suddenly, there's a quiet knock on the door.

Molly looks up and holds her breath. "Mom?"

"No, dear. It's Grandma."

"Oh!" Molly hasn't spoken to Grandma all day; she doesn't have a cell phone, and from what Mom told her, Grandma stayed isolated in her bedroom just like Molly.

"I'm coming in," Grandma says, and Molly hears the lock turn.

The door opens, and Grandma's frail figure appears. To Molly's relief, Grandma doesn't look ill at all. Seeing her makes Molly's heart grow several sizes.

"Grandma!" she exclaims, jumping up from the bed.

But Grandma stops her with an outstretched hand. "We can't touch, dear. Not yet. Not until I'm sure I'm not contagious anymore."

Molly frowns. "What do you mean, Grandma?"

Grandma darts a look back down the hallway, as though she's worried someone's listening. Then she steps inside the room and closes the door gently. To Molly's surprise, Grandma brought the key and now locks the door from the inside.

What is she afraid of?

The thought makes a cold shiver run down Molly's back.

"Now listen, dear," Grandma says, sounding even more serious than usual. "It's important you hear what I have to say and then you do as I tell you. Understood?"

"Sure, Grandma, but what—"

"No questions, dear. Not yet. Just listen."

Molly nods.

Grandma takes a deep breath, then begins talking. Molly listens, even though it feels very weird standing at opposite ends of the room like this.

"I caught the infection from Leo. But just like with Veronica, I didn't really get ill. The black stuff was in my hair, around my eyes, on my hands …" She shows both palms. They're pink and clean. "But now it's gone. I checked everywhere. And I'm feeling fine."

Molly feels a surge of relief. "That's great news, Grandma. It means Mom could also—"

"Please, dear. Don't interrupt. I'm not finished."

Molly clams up.

"You're right, it is good news. But we can't know if I'm still carrying the infection and could pass it to you. So we're going to stay ten feet apart at all times. No touching. That's very important. You understand?"

Molly swallows and nods.

"Good. Now, here's the bad news." Grandma takes a breath through her nose. "Your mother and your grandfather ... they'll end up like Leo."

Molly groans and covers her mouth. Even though she already knew it, it's still painful to hear it said outright.

"In fact, your grandfather is almost there. I just went to check on him, and he ..." Grandma stops talking. "Well, you don't need to hear the details. Suffice to say, he's very ill. And he's sleeping deeply now, just like your uncle Leo did."

Molly can't help herself. She asks, "Will Grandpa disappear, too?"

"I don't know. Frankly, I hope so. I think we were very lucky that your uncle did."

Molly frowns. "What are you talking about? How does that make us lucky that Uncle Leo—"

"I've been listening to the radio all day," Grandma cuts her off. Her tone is very firm now, her eyes bore into Molly's. "This is happening on the mainland, too. The infection is turning people into ... something else. Something dangerous. They haven't said just what it is, but we're in danger, Molly."

Molly's heart is beating fast. "I don't ... I don't understand ..."

"You don't need to. You just need to come with me."

"Where are we going?" Molly asks, gesturing towards the window. "The snow's still there, and Veronica has the snow scooter."

Grandma lowers her voice. "We're not leaving the house. We're going into the attic. We'll hide until the police get here. Hopefully, they won't find us up there."

"Who?"

Grandma doesn't answer; she doesn't need to. Her eyes tell.

"Oh, jeez," Molly whimpers. "Will Mom ... and Grandpa ... will they ... will they hurt us?"

"Not if we hide from them," Sylvia says, raising her eyebrows. "And we need to go now, before it's too late."

Molly takes a shaky breath. "Okay, Grandma."

Grandma nods once, then takes out something she's been hiding in her sleeve. Molly is shocked to see a huge carving knife. Grandma turns and unlocks the door. She listens for a moment before she opens it. Checking in both directions, she steps out into the hallway. She looks back briefly and whispers, "Don't touch the handle."

Molly goes to the door and peeks outside. The hallway is empty. The doors to Mom's and Grandpa's rooms are both closed.

Grandma heads for the living room, which means passing by Grandpa's door.

Molly follows her. She can't help but pause briefly by the door and listen. She expects to hear labored breathing. Instead, a gruff voice faintly resembling Grandpa's calls out: "Sylvia!"

Molly jumps and gives off a scream.

Grandma whirls around and stares at her.

"*Sylvia!*" Grandpa calls again. "*What did you do to me, you bitch?*"

Molly is terrified to hear Grandpa talk like this. Not only is his altered voice scary—she's also never heard him address Grandma this way.

"Come on," Grandma says to Molly, waving at her. "Keep moving."

"You think this'll hold me, Sylvia?" Grandpa roars, and Molly can hear him begin thrashing in there.

"Come *on!*" Grandma demands. "Move, Molly!"

Molly halfway realizes that Grandma did something to Grandpa while he slept. There's no time for questions, though, so she just hurries after Grandma, keeping her distance.

As they enter the living room, Grandma runs around the half wall separating the kitchen from the dining area. A couple of lights are on in here. Molly is hot on Grandma's heels, and she almost bumps into her as she stops abruptly.

"What is it, Grandma?"

Grandma doesn't answer. She's staring at something. Molly can't see what it is. As she steps to the side, she feels a cold gust of wind, and she notices one of the windows is open. It seems to have been forcedly opened from the outside, because the frame is broken, and snow is littering the floorboards. Following the snowy trail, Molly finally sees what made Grandma freeze up.

Right there, besides the couch, is her uncle Leo, staring back at them.

6

FELIX

OKAY, SO ... NOW what?

Felix is walking down the crowded sidewalk, glancing back every thirty seconds to make sure the soldiers aren't coming for him. They aren't. And there's very little risk they'll find him in the busy city.

He has no idea what to do now; he didn't plan that far ahead; he was just focused on getting away.

He's more than a hundred miles away from home, he's lost Pia, and he has no money, no transportation.

Even if he does get back home to his dad, what would happen then? No doubt the authorities will contact his father and explain the situation to him. That Felix is infected and needs to be taken into custody.

Will his dad believe Felix if he tells him otherwise? Or will he blindly trust the police?

Felix honestly doesn't know. But he can put out a feeler.

Still walking, he pulls out his phone and calls up his dad.

He answers on the third beep. *"What's up, Felix?"*

It's immediately clear from his dad's casual tone that he's not been informed about what's gone down.

"Hi, Dad. Uhm ... you busy?"

"Well, I'm at work, so yeah. But I can talk for five minutes if it's important?"

"It is," Felix mutters. "It definitely is."

His dad sighs. "*What now? Don't tell me you and Pia got in a fight ...*"

"No, it's nothing like that. But ... it's pretty bad news, Dad. You might wanna ... I don't know, brace yourself."

His dad falls quiet. "*What happened, son?*"

Felix takes a deep breath and looks back again. Still no one trailing him. He turns the corner and starts speaking in a low voice. He explains everything that's happened, beginning with the woman at the airport all the way to his escape—he alters that last part slightly so it sounds less dramatic, leaving out the stair truck and the soldiers chasing him. He makes it sound like he basically just snuck off.

When he's finally done talking, he waits for his dad's response. It's so quiet on the other end, he checks the phone's screen to make sure the call is still on.

"*I don't ... I don't know what to say, son ...*"

"Yeah, I know. It's insane."

"*So, it's some kind of contagion? They spoke about it on the news, but ... I mean, they said it was only way up in North Jutland.*"

"It was. Until the woman got on that plane and infected everybody."

"*Jesus Christ ... Pia ... are you sure she ...?*"

Felix can hear his dad swallow. "Yeah. I'm sorry, Dad."

"*I mean, are you **absolutely certain**? Couldn't she have slipped it somehow? Like you did?*"

"No. I saw her hand. She's ... definitely infected."

"*Fuck,*" his dad hisses. "*Fuck me ... But **you're** okay? You're sure you're okay?*"

"I am," Felix says, checking his hand. "Still nothing where she touched me. The cellophane did the trick."

"*Well, that's a relief,*" his dad says. "*Good thinking, son.*"

The compliment is so unlike his father, it catches Felix off guard, and he doesn't know what to say.

"I need to ... I need to call someone. Find out where Pia is. I need to go see her."

"No, Dad, you don't understand. They didn't just take them to the hospital. They're being isolated. That virus, or whatever it is ... it's very dangerous. It changes people, apparently. Turns them into monsters."

"Jesus, don't say that ..."

"But it's true. There's no way you get to visit Pia. And even if you did, you shouldn't."

"Look, she's my wife, and—"

"And she's gone, Dad! I know it's hard to understand, but ... unless they find a cure within, like, four hours, every single person on that plane is going to be transformed."

Felix expects his dad to get angry. To tell him off. But to his surprise, when his father speaks again, his voice is weak. "Oh, Christ ... this can't be happening. Not again. Not her, too."

Felix feels a stab to his heart. Accepting Pia's fate is fairly easy for Felix, because he didn't care too much about her and never really considered her part of the family. But his dad loves her very much. And he already lost his first wife in a pretty painful way.

"I'm really sorry, Dad."

A moment of silence.

"There's something else I need to ask you," Felix goes on.

His dad sniffs. "*What?*"

"Can I ... can I come home?"

Another pause.

"Why are you asking me that?"

"Well, because ... like I said, they're looking for me. The authorities. They'll want to put me in isolation like the others, because they don't believe I'm not infected. If they find me, they're gonna arrest me."

The pause is a little longer this time. Felix waits with bated breath.

"Well, if they think it's best to keep you under observation for a little while ..."

"No, Dad," Felix says, feeling his heart sink. "You don't get. They'll never let me go. Don't you get it? They have no idea what this is. They don't know how fast or slowly the infection comes on. They might keep me for months just to be sure."

"If they don't know how this thing acts, what makes you think that you do?"

The slight skeptical tone in Dad's voice makes Felix heart turn even harder. This was exactly what he feared. His father is once again trusting the authorities over him.

"Because I saw it with my own eyes, Dad. I saw how quickly the woman changed. She looked completely different on the plane than she did in the airport. And Pia ... the spot on her hand, it came on in less than thirty minutes. If I was infected, it would have shown by now."

"But you can't know that for sure, son. And you don't wanna risk infecting anybody else, do you? What if you did catch the thing and you're contagious? Did you ever stop to think about that?"

Felix stops and closes his eyes.

"You should turn yourself in," his dad goes on. *"Let them deal with it. Don't run around like a fugitive, putting others at risk."*

"Okay, Dad," Felix hears himself say.

"Good. You're doing the right thing, son." Felix can hear his dad has already moved on mentally to the next—and, to him, more important—subject. *"Look, I'm going to make some phone calls now. See if I can figure out where they're keeping Pia and how she's holding up. I'll call you back when I know more, okay?"*

"Okay, Dad," Felix says again, sounding mechanical.

"Thanks, son. Talk to you soon."

"Talk soon."

His dad ends the call, and Felix looks at his phone. He doubts very much they'll talk anytime soon.

It's clear to him that going home is out of the question, at least for now.

He had imagined that if he stays away for a few days, he might be able to prove to the authorities that he's not infected. But will him being asymptomatic after 48 hours be enough for them to accept it as proof? Very likely not.

And besides, now that he can't go home, where would he stay? He can't be outdoors, especially not at night. He'll freeze to death. And how will he get anything to eat? Steal something from a restaurant? That seems very risky.

There's only one place he can really go. One person who'll believe him and help him. That person is his mom. And the facility she's living at is only a few hours away.

7

MOLLY

SHE CAN SEE IT'S her uncle, although it's not easy to tell. If she hadn't known him her entire life, she probably wouldn't recognize him.

To say he's changed doesn't quite cut it. It looks more like he's been blended together with something else. Something from another world. Something straight out of a nightmare.

His shoulders are wide and boney, his hips narrow. His arms are so long, they reach his knees. His legs are longer, too, making him stoop forward in order to not bump his head against the wooden beams in the ceiling. His head is deformed; the back seems to have grown, and his forehead is bulging out. Not all the lights are on in the living room, and Molly is grateful for that. Yet she can still make out most of her uncle's features in the horrific face. Like his nose, which has shrunk and seems to be going away completely. He's only wearing boxers, so his skin is visible, and it no longer looks like human skin. For one thing, the color is off, and it looks harder and more leatherlike. Almost like the skin of a crocodile. At the same time, it's so thin and clings so tightly to his body, it's like a thin veneer covering the bones and veins just below.

His eyes are the worst part, though.

Shaped like almonds and crooked, they're too far apart, and they're completely unlike her uncle's friendly blue eyes. Instead, they're blank like crystal balls and seem to almost glow in the dark with an icy whiteness.

"Leavin', Mom?"

The words are so distorted, Molly almost can't understand them at first. Leo tilts his big head and widens his mouth in what looks like a smile.

"Leo," Grandma says, her voice stern but a little shaky at the same time. "Son. Please. The doctors can help you."

"Doctors," Leo repeats, breaking into a screeching, rattling laughter. Then he simply says, "No."

He takes a step forward, and Grandma says loudly, "Stay back, Leo. Don't come any closer."

Leo doesn't obey. He walks across the floor, moving more like a big insect than a person.

Molly whimpers and draws back a little. She wants to run back down the hallway, but she can hear Grandpa shouting and banging from his bedroom, and she suspects he'll come bursting out any second.

Her uncle apparently hadn't noticed her before, because she was hidden behind Grandma. He leans sideways and sends her an awful smile. She can tell his teeth are sharp like needles. "Hey, Molly."

"Don't talk to her," Grandma demands, sounding angry now. "Leave her alone."

Uncle Leo looks at Grandma, and his smile turns sour. Then he simply walks past her. Molly knows she should run away, or at the very least dive behind the half wall right next to her, but she can't move. She can only stand there and watch Leo approach. His bony frame towers over her as he comes close, and now she can see and smell the blood that's smeared all over his face and chest and hands. As though he's been bathing in it.

"Molly," he says again with that horrible voice, and what makes it even more frightening is that there's a trace of how Leo would say it, that warm, teasing tone he always used. "Little Molly." He reaches out a hand, and Molly gasps, and then her uncle jolts and stops.

His expression changes, and as he turns around, Molly can see the knife sticking out from his back. It's lodged between two ribs.

"Don't you touch her," Grandma hisses. Standing in front of Leo, she looks very small and frail and old. Yet her eyes are shooting fire up at him. "You take me if you have to, but you leave the girl alo—"

Grandma never gets to finish the sentence.

Leo lunges at her with a shrieking roar. It looks like a tiger attacking a baby deer. Grandma is tackled to the floor, and Leo basically tears her apart using his claws and teeth. Grandma doesn't scream, but Molly hears her groan with pain as Leo bites off chunks of her flesh and slashes her open with his nails.

Molly will never forget those sounds.

She blinks, feels a brief sensation of falling, and then everything turns black.

8

TIM

"CANNOT STOP IT; YOU will all perish."

The words are echoing in his mind as he drives down the highway. Helena is in the passenger seat, checking her phone now and then. Neither of them say much.

"He exploded, Tim. He fucking blew up."

For some reason, Tim keeps hearing Alan's and Lundbeck's voices, his memory replaying them over and over again. Now that he finally has nothing else that requires his immediate focus, he can feel something is trying to come to the surface.

"You cannot stop it; you will all perish."

There was something wrong with Alan's message. Or rather, Tim's translation. He hadn't gotten it right, not completely.

Tim is by no means an expert in linguistics, but he understands more or less how a language works: A word refers to a thing or action. String them together in a sentence, and you get something meaningful.

What Alan had uttered didn't work that way at all. It wasn't so much words as emotional outbursts, which is what made it so hard for Tim to discern.

The first part, "cannot," the idea that someone is unable to do something, that can mean a ton of different things, even in human language. But in Alan's tongue, there were even more variables to it. "Can," "will" and "want," as far as Tim could understand, are all the same word, only uttered in different ways. And who is being referred to also depends on how it's said.

So, in theory, instead of "You cannot stop it," Alan could have said, "They don't want to stop it," or "I won't stop it" or some other combination. Tim had gone with "can" because he picked up on a subtle feeling from Alan that told him "I could if I would, but ..."

And he's fairly certain he got that much right. The "can" part. What he misinterpreted was the who. Alan could be referring to them, or himself, or the goddamn prime minister, all depending on how he said it. Tim had assumed Alan was talking about them. That *they* couldn't stop what was happening. In reality, though, Tim now sits with the clear feeling that Alan had referred to himself. "*I* cannot stop it."

Second error. The word "perish."

Depending on the context, who's doing it, and how it's being said, that word has almost endless variations. On one end of the spectrum, it can mean very bad things, like "die," "go extinct," or "be annihilated." Tim got an ominous feeling from Alan when he said it. Which is why he misunderstood and went with "perish." On the other hand, it can be very neutral, like "dissolve," "hide," or simply "go away."

He believes that last one comes pretty damn close to what Alan was really saying.

So, what Tim took as, "You cannot stop it; you will all perish," probably was more like, "I cannot stop it; you need to get far away."

Which turns an ill-meant omen into a kind warning.

Alan knew what was going to happen to him. And whatever humanity was left in him desperately tried to communicate it and give them a heads-up.

"Dad?"

He blinks and looks at Helena. "Hmm?"

"Are you sure going back there is a good idea? I mean with what's happened up there."

"No, probably not," Tim admits. "But I need to get Buddy."

"Yeah, I know." She reaches up and touches the picture that's hanging from the rear mirror. It's a young woman, probably the girlfriend of the guy who owned the car before Tim stopped him in the parking lot and asked him friendlily to hand over the keys. "But where do we go from there?"

Tim looks at her. "What do you mean?"

"Well, if this is the end of the world, then shouldn't we go somewhere? That's usually what people do in the movies, anyway."

Tim grunts. "Where would you have us go?"

"I don't know. Australia? Somewhere the infection won't reach."

"You figure it won't reach Australia?" His question is earnest. "You think they can contain it?"

Helena looks out the windscreen and sighs. "Probably not."

"I don't think so, either. I think it's just a matter of time before this is everywhere on the globe. So we're probably not much safer on Barbados than we are back in my cabin." He chews the inside of his chin. "Besides, there's something I'd like to do when we get there."

"What's that?"

He realizes he said that last thought out loud. "Well ... this thing, it came from space. I saw a ... a rock. It came down and landed in the forest. That's where the spore is coming from." He glances sideways at her. "I haven't told anyone where it is."

"Not even the police?"

"No." He shrugs. "I figured the risk of anyone else coming across it was miniscule, so ..."

"What are you going to do to it then? Destroy it?"

"Nah, it's too late for that. I don't know, honestly. It's just that ... something tells me I need to go see the thing again."

Helena watches him for a moment, then she nods. "I think you should go with your instincts."

Tim can't help but smile. "You sound just like your mother now."

"That's usually said as an insult, you know?"

"I didn't mean it like that."

"No, I know."

They drive on in silence for half a minute.

Then Helena says quietly, "I really miss her."

"Me too," Tim says, squeezing the wheel. "Every minute of every day."

Another spell of silence. Tim feels her looking at him again.

"What?" he asks.

"There's ... there's something I need to tell you, Dad. I know it's kinda selfish, but ... it would really help me get it off my chest."

"Sure. What is it?"

"It's something really hurtful. Like, *really*."

Tim looks at her. She looks almost physically sick with concern. "Look, it's okay, honey. I can take it. There's nothing you can say that'll hurt my feelings, believe me."

"Really?"

"Really. Hit me."

Helena presses her lips together, then says, "I wished it had been you instead of her." She breaks into tears.

Tim is stunned for a few seconds. Then he exclaims, "That's it? That's all?"

"Yeah," Helena sobs, looking at him through her fingers. "I'm so sorry, Dad. I couldn't help feeling that way. I know it's horrible, but—"

Tim gives a snort of laughter. "Look, I get it. Trust me, honey, I've had that same wish a million times. If I could switch places with her, I would. In a heartbeat."

Helena stops crying and eyes him. "Seriously?"

"Oh, absolutely. The world would be much better off with her than with me."

"Well ... that's why I thought of it just now." She exhales shakily. "I don't think that's true. Not anymore. I mean, for one thing, you saved me."

"Yeah, but ..."

"And all those things you did to help the police. No one else could have done that."

"Lotta good it did," Tim mutters.

Helena doesn't seem to hear him. "I thought about it," she goes on, "and I think that's why the woman came for me, you know? It wasn't just random. She wanted to kill me to try and hurt you. To get you to stop fighting them."

Tim almost drops his jaw. It's like Helena has read his mind. "I think ... I think you're right."

"Yeah, and ... that's gotta be because they know you're very dangerous to them, right? I don't just mean because you can kick their asses, I mean ... something about you scares them. I think they know something about you we don't."

"Like what?"

Helena shrugs, then says earnestly, "Like how you're the only one who can save the world."

Tim scoffs. "I think you're reading too much into it now, honey."

"Maybe. But still ... that awful wish I used to carry around ..." She looks at him, and her eyes fill up with tears again. "I can feel it's completely gone."

Tim swallows and manages to smile back. "Thanks, sweetie."

His hand is resting on the gear lever. Helena places her hand on top of it. Less than half size of his, it's warm and soft. They stop talking and drive on. This time, the silence feels good.

9

MOLLY

SHE BLINKS HER EYES open and finds herself staring at the ceiling.

What happened?

She can hear wet smacking noises somewhere nearby. She looks to the side and realizes she's lying flat on her back on the floor.

Did I faint?

A throbbing pain in the back of her head seems to confirm the thought. Molly has no idea how much time has passed. How long she's been lying here. Could be ten minutes. Could be two seconds.

I should get up. I should run away.

She's not sure why, though. But for some reason, she feels like she's in danger.

She looks to the other side, and she sees something she doesn't compute at first. It's her uncle Leo—although he's hard to recognize. He's sitting over Grandma—or what's left of her—chowing away, producing the sticky noises mixed with satisfied grunts.

With a burning hot wave of fear, it all comes back to her.

She tries to get up, but her arms and legs don't really want to cooperate. They're fine with lying here. Even though

Molly knows that means she'll get eaten, too. As soon as Leo is done with Grandma, he'll come for her.

Her eyes catch something up above. Between two beams is a hatch. It's closed, but a string dangles from it.

That's where Grandma wanted us to go.

It's as though the thought makes her able to move again. Sitting up, the headache gets a little worse, but Molly ignores it. The sounds become louder too, as her mind clears up somewhat. She glances briefly over at Leo. He's got his back to her, and he's still preoccupied.

Molly gets to her feet and pulls herself up onto the half wall. It's just wide enough that she can stand on it. Molly does gymnastics at school, so she's fairly strong and agile, and even though she can't reach the beam, it only requires a little jump. She concentrates, takes off, and grabs hold of the beam. Hoisting herself up, she places herself astride it and looks down briefly.

Leo has slowed down the eating. He leans back and wipes at his mouth with the back of his hand, causing blood and strings of flesh to splatter to the floor. Grandma is little more than a messy pile of meat and bones. She looks less like a person and more like an apple someone dropped on the ground and now it's been hollowed out by a swarm of hungry insects.

Leo looks to the place where Molly stood. Seeing her gone, he jumps to his feet and runs around the half wall.

"Molly?" he calls out, causing her to jump. She holds her breath. The string to the hatch is dangling inches from her face, but she can't pull it. Leo will hear her. So, she just sits completely still, praying he won't look up.

He comes back around and stops almost right below her. He sniffs loudly and turns his head like an owl, scanning the room.

"Smell you, Molly," he breathes. "Close ..."

Molly feels like screaming and crying, but she bites down hard and swallows it all. Her arms and legs start to shiver violently.

It feels like Leo is about to look up—or maybe it's just something Molly imagines—either way, he's interrupted when there comes a bump from the hallway. Grandpa's voice comes from his bedroom: "Sylvia!"

Leo, apparently curious, goes over to look down the hallway. He doesn't quite leave the living room, but he's far enough away that Molly dares to reach up and pull the string. There comes a low click as some kind of mechanism allows the hatch to open a crack. Molly freezes and turns her head slowly to look in Leo's direction.

He obviously heard her, because he comes striding back across the floor. He stops again right below, whipping his head back and forth. "*Molly!*" he roars out, his voice breaking into that awful, whining tone. It's like nails on a chalkboard, and Molly feels an icy shiver run down her back.

Leo breathes like a bull, then he suddenly grabs the couch and flips it over like it was made of Styrofoam. Then he kicks over the coffee table.

Molly is shocked, but she also knows she needs to take advantage of the noise Leo is making. She pulls the hatch down almost to vertical, and as she does, a batch of dust slides off it and drizzles down like snow. Molly freezes and stares at the shower, afraid that Leo will notice. But he's too busy ripping down the curtains. So, she allows herself to breathe again. Then she sticks her head through the opening and stands up on the beam. She glances around quickly, seeing a dark, dusty attic. It's empty save for a few old cardboard boxes and a mattress wrapped in plastic. She can still hear Leo tearing the room apart below, clearly still not aware that she's right overhead, and she feels a wild elation as she realizes she's actually going to get away. As soon as she's up, she can close the hatch behind her, and Leo probably won't notice the dust that has settled on the floor by now, which is the only thing that'll reveal her hiding place.

She hoists herself up, and, reaching down, she gently closes her hatch. When there's only a two-inch opening left, she peeks down to see what Leo's doing. He's moved on to the kitchen area and is tearing open cupboards. Then Molly closes the hatch all the way, and it shuts with that same little click.

She looks around again, her eyes adjusting to the darkness. There's one tiny window at the far end, a pale, gray light coming through it. Getting to her feet, Molly walks slowly towards it, making sure to tread lightly so that the old floorboards won't give off any sounds and reveal her.

I did it, she thinks, feeling a smile tug at her mouth. *I got away. He'll never find me up here. I can just stay here and—*

Something black with wings comes out of the darkness and heads right for her face.

It happens so fast and so unexpectedly, Molly can't help but scream out in shock, and she reflexively throws up her hands as the strange, birdlike creature whisks close by her hair. She stares after it as it flies on down to the other end of the attic and disappears once again in the darkness.

That was a bat, Molly thinks, her heart thumping away. *I've never seen one before.*

She doesn't get any more time to worry about the animal, though. Because she notices at that moment how it's completely quiet below.

Molly holds her breath and listens.

Footsteps. Coming closer. Stopping.

A long pause.

Sniffing.

Then, Leo's voice, right below the hatch, low and distorted and terrifying: "Clever girl ..."

10

VERONICA

SHE FINALLY SPOTS THE cabin up ahead.

It feels like she's been driving all night, yet the sunset is clearly still hours away.

The cabin is dark except for a low light in the living room windows. There are three of them, and they're the old-fashioned kind with thick muntins dividing them into smaller parts. Which is why Veronica already from a distance can see something is wrong with one of the windows—the muntins are gone. So is the glass and the frame.

She immediately kills the engine and jumps off the scooter. Dropping the helmet and gloves in the snow, she brings the gun and runs the last stretch to the house, feeling her heart gear up. She approaches the broken window and can immediately tell it's been broken from the outside, because all the shards of glass and pieces of wood are *inside*.

She looks into the living room and finds it a complete mess. Every piece of furniture has been flipped over. In the middle of the room is Leo. She immediately recognizes him. He's standing still, apparently listening, looking up at the ceiling. Veronica raises the gun to her shoulder.

"Clever girl …" Leo whispers, his voice all wrong.

Then, just as Veronica is about to pull the trigger, he leaps into the air and crashes through the ceiling. His thin legs dangle for a moment, before he pulls them up too and disappears into the attic. Someone screams up there. A girl. Molly.

"Shit," Veronica hisses, climbing through the broken window as fast as she can.

She runs to the place where Leo went up, and she sees a broken hatch. She can't see him up there, but she hears him whisper: "Molly."

Veronica feels panic grip her. She might be too late. She considers calling out for Leo to distract him, but she still thinks the element of surprise will give both her and Molly a better chance of surviving, so she keeps quiet.

The ceiling beams are just out of her reach, but there's a tipped-over chair right next to her. She stands it upright, flings the gun over her shoulder, steps onto the chair, grabs the beam and climbs up. Standing on the beam, she's able to stick her head and upper body through the hole.

As she does, she sees Leo with his back to her. Molly is on the floor in front of him, on her back, completely exposed.

Veronica yanks the sling over her head, not taking her eyes off Leo. It feels like she's moving in slow motion. Every second, Leo can throw himself on the girl, and it'll be too late. Molly whimpers with fear. Just as it looks like Leo's about to attack her, Veronica shoulders the gun and calls out: "*Leo!*"

11

MOLLY

SHE CAN'T MOVE. IT'S like she's turned into a marble statue.

For a painfully long moment, Molly can only stand there, holding her breath, listening, hoping that Leo didn't figure out where she is. Her eyes are fixed on the hatch only ten feet away.

Then, suddenly, the hatch breaks open with a loud crash, as Leo thrusts his upper body through it.

Molly screams and reels back, her heels bumping into something. She falls over one of the cardboard boxes, tipping it over as she lands on her butt. She lifts her head and looks over the box to see Leo climb into the attic and get to his feet. The dim glow coming up through the opening makes her uncle look even more alien as he brushes pieces of the broken hatch off his shoulders and looks around the attic.

In a stroke of luck, the cardboard box is actually hiding Molly from view—as long as she stays flat on her back. She notices a few things that have spilled out from it. It's an old sewing machine, a couple of balls of yarn, and a pair of heavy metal scissors.

Molly stares at Leo as he scans the room, trying to find her. His head stops as his eyes land on her, and he gives off a long breath. "Molly," he whispers.

Molly sits up and goes for the scissors.

Leo lunges for her.

She manages to grab the scissors and hold them up just as Leo leans over the cardboard box. He grabs her by the shoulders, probably intending to lift her up, but he stops as the blade pierces his skin and slides in just below his collar bone.

Molly didn't try to stab him—she simply raised the scissors in an effort to shield herself and ward him off. Feeling it go into Leo's chest, she lets go of it with a gasp.

Leo also lets go of her and looks down at the scissors. He doesn't scream out like Molly anticipated. He simply grabs the handles and yanks the scissors back out with a grunt of pain. Looking briefly at the blades, which are all dark from blood now, he flings it across the floor. Then he glares down at Molly, and his eyes are full of rage.

Molly screams as loud as she can as Leo bends over her again—at least she tries to, but all that comes out is a hoarse whimper.

"*Leo!*"

A voice Molly recognizes.

Veronica's voice.

Leo spins around.

Molly stretches her neck.

Veronica's torso is sticking up through the opening. She's holding a gun against her shoulder. The barrel is aimed at Leo, and her head is slightly tilted.

The gun flashes, and then comes a sound so loud, Molly is sure the entire roof is ripped off the house.

The roof stays in place, though. The only thing moving is Leo, who's thrust back as though someone kicked him hard in the chest. He steps on the cardboard box and almost falls on top of Molly. He manages to only go down on his knees before he gives off a loud roar—at least Molly assumes he does, because his mouth is wide open, and spittle flies from his lips as he glares at Veronica. Then he takes off towards her, one of his arms hanging weirdly low, and then there's another flash from the gun, another ear-piercing explosion, and Leo is pushed back again. This time, hard enough that he lands on his back and doesn't immediately try to get back up.

Molly just sits there, covering her ears, staring at her uncle. He's still moving, but he's clearly badly hurt, and it's only now Molly realizes that Veronica used the gun to shoot him.

Veronica climbs all the way up, but she doesn't go to Leo right away. Molly sees her lower the gun, reach for her jacket pocket, and fiddle with something. Molly tries to say her name, tries to call for her, but she's not sure the words come out right; she can't really hear them.

Veronica raises the gun back up to her shoulder and steps forward just as Leo manages to roll over and get to his hands and knees.

He doesn't get any farther than that, though. Because Veronica stops, takes careful aim, and shoots him through the back of the head.

Molly sees Leo's face come off and land on the floor half a second before he collapses down on top of it.

Then she once again sees blackness.

12

VERONICA

VERONICA JUST STANDS THERE for twenty seconds or so, breathing hard—she feels the air going in and out, but she can't hear it.

She keeps the gun aimed at Leo, ready for another shot. He doesn't move a muscle. She didn't think he would; the pellets went straight through his skull. Whatever he's turned into, surely he can't function with a wasted brain.

When she's satisfied that Leo really is dead, she turns around and goes back to the hatch. She still keeps the gun ready. If anybody else is in the house, they obviously heard the gunshots.

Crouching down, she scans the room. No one's there.

She gets back up and goes to Molly. The girl is still lying flat on her back and hasn't moved. For an awful second, Veronica fears she might have hit her too—she definitely was within range of the first shot, but Veronica had to take it and trust her aim.

But she can't see any wounds or blood. The girl is pale but seems to be breathing just fine.

She just passed out. No wonder.

Putting the gun on the floor, Veronica touches Molly's shoulder, shaking her gently.

The girl smacks her lips and turns her head, but doesn't open her eyes. Veronica shakes her a bit harder and says her name—even though Molly's hearing is probably shot just like her own.

But it works. The girl blinks her eyes open and focuses on Veronica. She sits up and grabs her in a tight hug.

"We shouldn't touch," Veronica tells her, taking her arms away. "I might still be contagious, we don't know." She smiles at the girl. "But I'm really glad to see you. Are you OK?"

Molly nods. "I'm not hurt."

"Did Leo touch you?"

She shakes her head. "Not my skin, anyway. Thank you, Veronica. Thank you so much." The girl begins weeping, hiding her face in her hands.

"It's all right, sweetie," Veronica says, caressing her back. She allows her a minute to breathe. She really wants to get back down, not least to get away from Leo, who's reeking of blood and brain and citrus. But the girl has been through a lot. "Can you tell me what happened while I was away?"

Veronica's hearing is slowly improving, though there's still a shrill ringing, as she listens to the girl's mumbling, sobbing account of what went down. It gives her the chills.

"Jeez," she says. "I'm so sorry you had to go through all that. I'm sorry I left you, Molly."

The girl just nods. "It's okay. I get why you had to." She glances over at Leo. "But … did you have to …? Don't you think maybe Uncle Leo could've been … I don't know, like, cured?"

Veronica shakes her head. "I really don't think so, no. Even if he could have been, I had no choice. He was going to hurt you if I didn't stop him."

Molly takes a shaky breath, then whispers, "I guess you're right."

"So, your grandma ...?"

Molly nods towards the hatch. "She's right down there. Didn't you see her?"

"No, I didn't. I was in a hurry. But she's dead?"

"Definitely."

Veronica can't help but recall the woman in the bathtub, and she knows she needs to be careful. "All right," she says. "Come on, Molly. Let's get down from here. We need to leave."

"What, why?"

Veronica helps her up, making sure their skin doesn't touch. "It's not safe here. You told me your grandpa and your mother are still in the house, right?"

She leads Molly to the hatch. Checking again, she finds the living room still empty. She climbs down and jumps onto the floor. Immediately panning the gun around, she makes sure no one's hiding anywhere, ready to pounce on her. The only thing she can hear is the wind coming in through the broken window, and something which could be an engine, but very far off. Looking down, she notices what she missed coming in; Sylvia's remains are mostly hidden under the flipped-over coffee table. One of her thin hands is sticking out. She looks more like the old guy, and Veronica trusts that she really is dead.

"Okay, it's safe to come down, Molly," she whispers. "But try to be quiet, all right?"

The girl climbs down with surprising ease, landing on the floor without needing Veronica's help. She looks towards the window. "What's that? Is that ... a car coming?"

Veronica is aware that the sound of the engine has grown louder. "I think it might be the medics," she says. "It could be a few minutes more before they're here. We need to find out how your grandpa and your mom are doing. But I want you to stay here while I do it. Find someplace to hide. Can you do that?"

Molly nods, going to the kitchen area. She ducks down and slips into an already open cupboard, then closes the door.

"Good girl," Veronica mumbles, shouldering the shotgun, but keeping it at a forty-five-degree angle as she slips down the hallway.

Reaching Flemming's room first, she stops and listens for thirty seconds. The helicopter—Veronica is convinced by now that that's what the sound is—by now is pretty loud, and she can't really discern any noises coming from the room. The key is in the lock, and she turns it with a click, then steps back and raises the gun. Another thirty seconds pass. Nothing happens. Veronica reaches out a hand and opens the door a crack. Then she uses the barrel to push it open all the way, while she steps back again.

She can't see the entire room from out here, but she doesn't have to in order to figure out what's happened.

The bed is in disarray. Flemming clearly lied here minutes ago; there's a big, sweaty depression in the mattress. The pillow and blanket are both on the floor. Still clinging to the sides of the table are strips of duct tape. They appear to have been chewed or ripped through. The window is open, the curtain dancing in the breeze.

Veronica decides not to turn on the lights; her eyes are adjusted to the darkness, and she risks blinding herself.

So, she steps inside and looks around. There are only two possible places a guy Flemming's size could be hiding: inside the wardrobe and under the bed.

Veronica opens the closet door. Only clothes and linens.

She crouches down and looks under the bed. Nothing.

Finally, she goes to window and sees exactly what she expected: big, barefooted prints leading away from the house.

The sound of the helicopter is loud now, and Veronica sees a yellow light a few hundred yards overhead. It's quickly headed this way.

She goes back to the hallway and approaches Alice's room. She remembers that her sister-in-law wasn't as far advanced as Flemming when Veronica left the cabin. So it's more likely that she's still in her room.

Just like Flemming's door, this one is locked too, the key still in the hole.

Veronica goes through the same procedure. As she pushes open the door, she immediately sees Alice.

Sylvia did a decent job of securing her husband and daughter to their beds, but it seems she ran out of duct tape with Alice, and so she resorted to using a robe and a piece of extension cord for the lower half of her body.

"Alice?" Veronica asks—talking loudly in order for her sister-in-law to hear her over the roar of the helicopter, now seemingly right overhead. "Alice, can you hear me?"

Alice appears to be sleeping. But she could be faking it.

Veronica steps closer. Her sister-in-law's face is pale and almost serene in the darkness. No trace of the black stuff. She's clearly passed the critical stage and has entered the deep, coma-like sleep Veronica found Leo in. Alice's body is hidden under the duvet, but looking closer at her face, Veronica can tell her features have been altered slightly.

There's no way back for her, Veronica thinks, a tightness settling in her chest. *I ought to shoot her right here and now.*

But she can't bring herself to do it. Not with Molly in the other room. Not as long as there's a tiny hope of saving Alice. The helicopter sounds like it's touched down on the other side of the house, and the engine is slowing down. Perhaps the doctors have figured out something. Perhaps they're bringing a cure. Veronica doesn't think it's likely, but she makes the decision to let Alice have that last, tiny hope.

So, she leaves her and goes to greet the medics.

13

VERONICA

SHE GOES TO THE kitchen, opens the cupboard and tells Molly to stay put for now.

"What about my mom, Veronica?" the girl asks.

"She's sleeping," Veronica tells her with a quick smile. "Now, keep quiet until I come back. Don't open for anyone else. Okay?"

The girl nods. Veronica closes the cupboard and exits the cabin through the front door.

The helicopter has landed on a relatively flat area of the garden. The rotors are still slowing down as Veronica steps outside. Sharp floodlights are beaming from the aircraft in every direction, turning the immediate surroundings into day. Snow is being hurled through the air and whipped against her face. She squints and tries to see the helicopter. It's hard, but she makes out a person jumping out of the door.

"Who are you?" a male voice calls out—sounding slightly muffled. "Why are you armed? Put down the gun, please!"

Veronica isn't exactly aiming at the helicopter, but she is instinctively keeping it ready. "Are you guys doctors?" she calls back.

"Yes! We've come to help. You have three sick people in there, right?"

"Well, there's only one left," Veronica says. "But you've come to the right place."

A brief pause. The rotors have almost stopped now and the snow is settling down. Veronica darts a look around herself. She's very aware that Flemming is out here somewhere. It's pretty likely that he took off like Leo did. But it's also possible that he heard the helicopter coming and stuck around.

"What do you mean, only one left?" the guy asks. "What happened to the others?"

"One of them died. The other wandered off."

"Wandered off? Just like that?"

"Can you please put down the weapon?" another voice calls, and Veronica sees a second guy join the other in the sea of lights. He's carrying a large suitcase.

Veronica secures the gun and slings it over her shoulder. One of the medics comes closer as the rotors finally stop completely, leaving the night quiet once more. The other guy has gone back into the helicopter, and some of the lights are turned off, leaving the area still well lit, but no longer blinding.

Veronica finally sees the aircraft properly. It's yellow with red stripes on top of it, and the door is open, revealing a lot of medical equipment. To Veronica's pleasant surprise, they're both wearing full hazmat suits, complete with breathing apparatuses.

The closest one of them reaches Veronica and greets her with a nod. He appears to be not much older than her. "I'm Jeppe."

"Veronica Steen. Glad to see you guys are taking it seriously."

"From what you told us, we have to assume it's the Nigrum fungus."

Veronica feels her heart leap. "You know what it is?"

Jeppe turns his head to look back as his colleague comes through the snow to join him. The second guy is shorter and broader and apparently a little older. "So, what's the status?" he asks. "Can we go inside, please? I'm already freezing."

They start for the house.

"It was my father-in-law who called you," Veronica tells them over her shoulder. "Flemming Brun. He was infected, as were his son, his daughter, and his wife."

"Flemming caught it first?" Jeppe asks, as they step inside.

"No," Veronica says, turning to look at them, and in a split-second, she decides to lie. "Leo did. His son. He infected the others."

"What about you?" the other medic asks, as though immediately reading her mind.

"I was very careful," Veronica tells him coolly.

Jeppe looks around the hall. "Anyone else been here who didn't catch the infection?" he asks.

Once again, without skipping a beat, Veronica lies. "No. No one else."

She surprises herself. She always considered herself a truthful person. One who kept true to her word. One who didn't lie. But these past few days have proved her wrong. Keeping quiet about her cancer diagnosis was one thing; that's a private matter, and not something she's obligated to announce right away. She might have told Leo in her own time—had the world gone on as usual and not turned into this insane science fiction movie she finds herself in.

But not telling Leo about the infection? And, once he fell ill, not admitting right away that she was the cause of it? What was that about? Protecting her own ass? That isn't like her.

Add to that, now she's blatantly lying to the medics about this obviously incredibly dangerous disease.

Veronica is flushed with a feeling of not knowing herself any more.

And yet ... yet she doesn't second-guess her decision.

Her gut tells her she's right to keep Molly and her own brief infection a secret—at least for now. At least until she knows how the medics treat Alice.

She notices the second medic—the one who didn't give her a name—is eyeing her through the visor. "It's just that, before we landed, I noticed a snow scooter on the other side of the house. Tracks leading this way."

"That's me," Veronica says promptly. "I left to try and get help from the neighbors." She shrugs. "Never reached them. It was snowing so badly, I couldn't see where I was, so I turned back after five minutes."

"Huh," the guy says. "What's with the shotgun then?"

This time, Veronica doesn't need to lie. "It's for protection. Leo, the guy who caught it first ... he turned extremely violent. I couldn't be sure Flemming or Alice wouldn't too."

The medics exchange a look, but it's not one of surprise; from what Veronica can see of their faces, they look grim.

"You guys knew that already?" she asks. "That they become dangerous once the infection is far enough along?"

"How much have you heard of what's going on on the mainland?" Jeppe asks.

"Look," the other one cuts him off, "we don't have time to stand around talking. Time is of the essence here. Who's the person that's left?"

"Alice," Veronica says, leading them into the living room. "She's tied to her bed. Last time I checked on her, she was still sleeping. It's right down—"

"Jesus Christ," the older medic exclaims, putting down the suitcase. "What happened in here?"

Veronica looks around at the mess. "It's a long story, but, as I said ... Leo turned violent. I had to ... I had to shoot him."

Both men look at her, and it's all Veronica can do not to take a step back. The gun is still sitting on her back. She suddenly wishes she'd kept it in her hands.

"You shot him?" Jeppe repeats.

"I had no choice. He was going to kill me."

The other medic starts moving around the room a little. He tries to make it look casual, but Veronica can feel he's suddenly tense. They all are.

"Okay," Jeppe says, nodding. "Okay, well ... the police are on their way. They'll have to deal with that. Right, Frank?"

Frank doesn't answer. He seems to have found something. He's looking at the coffee table.

"What is it?" Jeppe asks.

"Is this him?" Frank asks, addressing Veronica. "Is this Leo Brun?"

Veronica turns towards him, discreetly slipping the gun strap over her head as she does. "No, that's not him. That's his mother, Sylvia Brun. He attacked her and ate her ... as you can probably tell."

"All right," Frank says, surprising Veronica by accepting her answer without further inquiry. "We're not here for the dead. Show us to Alice, please. Hopefully, we can still help her."

Veronica is holding on to the strap, which is sitting on her right shoulder now, so that the gun is ready to come off completely. She's hoping that the guys won't notice. "Sure," she says, pointing towards the hallway. "It's the last room on the left."

They're about to leave, when there comes a sound from the kitchen. Veronica whirls around to see Molly come out of the cupboard.

"Molly! I told you to stay in there ..."

The girl was headed for her, but now stops dead in her tracks, as though Veronica had slapped her.

"It's not safe out here," Veronica tells her—and even as she's talking, she senses Jeppe approaching fast from the side. She turns on him and slips the gun off her shoulder in one fluent motion. "Stay back!"

Jeppe stops, but his eyes flicker, and Veronica sees Frank coming from the other side too late. He smacks the barrel of the gun down and grabs her in a sideways bear hug. Lifting her off the ground, he twists her so that her legs swing up, and then he slams her down her back.

The air is knocked from her lungs, and the gun is ripped from her hands. Before Veronica can regain her bearings, she's flipped over on her belly, a knee is places between her shoulder blades, and her wrists are squeezed together behind her back. She's still heaving for air, her lungs unwilling to draw in a proper breath, and she can hear Molly scream.

"I didn't ... didn't do anything," Veronica croaks.

"Oh, yeah?" Frank hisses in her ear. "You just confessed to murder, you crazy bitch."

"Self ... defense ..." She wants to say something else, but she can't.

"No one else here?" he asks, his voice shaking from fear or anger or both. "What else did you lie about? Huh?"

"Why would you pull the gun on me if you're innocent?" Jeppe asks from somewhere nearby.

Veronica doesn't have an answer that won't sound like another lie.

"What'll we find if we search this place, huh?" Frank demands. "Tell me!"

"Alice ... in last room," Veronica groans, finally starting to breathe again. "Leo ... attic. Dead."

"We can't trust a word she says anyway," Frank concludes. "Get me something to tie her down with, Bille. Hurry!"

Veronica lifts her head just enough to see the place where Molly was. The girl's gone now. Probably got scared by the fighting and went to hide somewhere.

Jeppe comes over with a nylon strap, and Frank pulls her up, sits her down in Sylvia's armchair and runs a strap around her chest once, fixing her to the chair. Then he secures both her wrists to the armrests.

"You're staying there until the cops show up," he informs her, then turns towards Jeppe. "Give me the gun."

The younger medic is holding the weapon awkwardly. He seems to have noticed something from down the hallway.

"Hey, Bille!" Frank calls out in a whisper-shout. "What is it?"

Jeppe looks at him. "I think I heard something."

"The girl?"

"No, I ... I don't think so."

Frank goes to him and takes the weapon. It's clearly not his first time handling a gun. He checks both chambers, muttering angrily. "Said they'd be here long before us. Stupid fucking cops. Doing *their* damn work."

"We should have turned around like Poulsen told us," Jeppe interjects.

"Coulda, shoulda, woulda," Frank snarls. "We're here now, and we're dealing with it."

The younger medic glances at Veronica. He doesn't look comfortable, but at least he's not running away.

"Please," Veronica says, grateful to be able to fill her lungs again. "You don't need to do this. Untie me, and I'll cooperate."

Frank just scoffs. "I'll go check the rest of the cabin. You stay here, Bille. And don't you dare feel sorry for her and let her loose." He then shoulders the gun and disappears down the hallway.

14

MOLLY

SHE CLOSES THE DOOR as quietly as she can.

It's dark in the room, and it's awfully cold. There's also a heavy smell of lemons in the air. Molly ignores it and focuses on getting the key into the hole. She twists it and hears the lock snap into place.

Then she steps back, holding her breath, staring at the door. She listens. She can hear a scuffle from the living room. The medics shout. But no one comes down the hallway. No one's chasing Molly. She feels a little relieved, even though she's still worried for Veronica. Why did she even point the gun at the doctors? Didn't she trust them? They'd come to help, so why—

A grunt makes her whirl around.

She almost forgot about Mom.

Seeing her there on the bed, tied down with ropes and duct tape, her face pale in the dim gray light from the window, it sends a mixture of feelings through Molly.

On the one hand, she knows Mom is sick. That the strange disease has infected her.

But on the other, she looks almost like her old self. As though she's only sleeping. Like Snow White in the glass coffin.

A cold wind makes the curtains move, and Molly shivers. She can see her own breath.

It's quieter from the living room now. The doctors are talking with each other, but no longer shouting. Veronica's voice, too.

Did they make peace?

Molly doubts it. She saw the older medic grab Veronica and slam her into the floor. It's more likely that they—

Mom grunts again. A nerve twitches under her right eye.

Molly steps a little closer. "Mom?" she whispers. "Are you awake?"

There are no traces of the black stuff left—which is a big relief to Molly. From what she heard the grown-ups talk about, Leo was a pretty awful sight when he was at the sickest.

But then the black stuff went away.

And they all thought—hoped—he was better.

He wasn't.

But Veronica had the infection, too. The black stuff grew on her, too. And it went away, too. And she was better. Perfectly normal.

Is that what has happened to Mom? Or is she like Leo now?

The mere thought of Mom running around like some overgrown insect, razor-sharp teeth, barely able to talk ... it's all Molly can do not to burst into tears.

She forces herself to take one more step, stopping right next to the bed. She leans a little forward to see Mom's face better. She tries hard to figure out whether Mom looks okay or not. She can still vividly recall Leo's features as he came for her in the attic. He didn't look like himself—well, he did, but he was changed. His chin, his jaw, his nose ... but most obvious were his eyes.

Mom's face doesn't seem changed. Her skin is still the right color. And her eyes are closed. Molly can tell they're moving slowly back and forth below the eyelids. As though Mom's dreaming.

Molly's heart is pounding so hard, she can hear it inside her ears.

Is she all right? Is she still my mom?

Footsteps coming down the hallway. They're walking slow. They sound too heavy to be Veronica. They stop. A handle is turned, a door opens.

Molly stands absolutely still and listens.

After thirty seconds or so, the footsteps come again. She counts five or six of them. Then they stop once more. Another handle rattles, another door opens.

It's one of the medics, Molly realizes. *He's checking all the rooms.*

The door is locked, but Molly isn't sure that'll keep him out. She's seen in the movies how a door can be kicked in. What will he do when he finds Molly here?

Mom gives off another sound, and Molly looks at her. Her eyes have stopped moving. She's breathing a little deeper now. Is she waking up?

Molly recalls how different Leo's hands were. She looks down to check Mom's hand. They look normal. Perhaps a bit too thin, and the nails seem a few millimeters longer than usual, but Mom could have just forgot to cut them.

There's one other way to find out for sure ...

Molly leans over the bed, reaches out her hand, and, with a shaking thumb, she gently pulls Mom's eyelid up.

She only gets Mom's eye halfway open before someone suddenly grabs the door handle and yanks it hard. Molly jumps and almost screams out.

"I know you're in there, girl," the medic says. "Unlock the door, please."

Molly doesn't know what to do. She clasps both hands over her mouth, as though she's afraid it might say something without her consent.

The medic bangs on the door. "Open the door, girl. Your mom is in there too, right? I know she's sick. I can help her."

Can he? Or is it just something he says to get Molly to open?

Molly is torn. Should she open it? Should she jump out the window? Should she hide in the cupboard?

The medic keeps knocking, keeps telling her to unlock the door, when suddenly ...

"Psst."

Molly whips around and stares toward the window. She expects someone to be there, but no one is.

"Molly."

She looks down and gasps out loud.

Mom's eyes are open. They still look like Mom's eyes. At least a little. But the blue is definitely fading.

"Mom," Molly breathes, feeling like her knees are about to buckle.

"It's okay," Mom whispers. "Sssssh." She winks at Molly, smiles, then closes her eyes again.

Then the door bursts open with a loud crash.

15

FRANK

HE TAKES A STEP back, measures the distance, then lunges forward leading with the sole of his right boot. It connects with the door right below the handle, and it's enough to break the lock and make the door fly open.

He immediately whips the gun around, expecting the worst.

What he sees in the dark room, though, isn't exactly anything threatening.

The girl is by the bed, staring at him with huge, shocked eyes. Evidently she was checking on the woman in the bed when Frank kicked in the door. The woman is secured to the bed just like the person in the next room over had been, before they got free. Her eyes are closed, and she must be unconscious since the noise from the door didn't stir her.

"It's okay," Frank tells the girl, lowering the gun a little. "I'm a doctor. I've come to help."

The girl doesn't say anything. She steps a little to the side, obviously wanting to get away from Frank, but not wanting to abandon the woman in the bed.

"Is that your mom, girl?" he asks, fumbling for the light switch.

The girl nods.

"What's your name?"

He finds the switch and flips it. The lights come on, revealing that the room appears to be empty. There's a tall cupboard, and someone could be hiding under the bed. But Frank doubts it. He feels safe enough to place the gun in the strap over his shoulder. He steps inside and repeats the question.

"M ... Molly," she says in a thin voice.

"Okay, Molly. You don't need to run away, and you don't need to be scared of me. My name's Frank. Your grandfather called for a doctor, so I've come to help. Don't let the suit and the mask scare you—it's just a precaution." He gestures towards the hallway. "The reason we got a little ... rough with Veronica back there was that she had this gun, and we weren't sure whether she was going to use it on us. The police are on their way, and they would have done the same thing. It's not legal to point a gun at anybody. You understand that, right?"

The girl nods again, but she doesn't exactly look convinced. Her eyes keep going from Frank to the woman.

"I'm sure you're worried about your mom," he goes on, coming properly into the room now. "Veronica told us she caught that weird disease that makes this black stuff grow on you—is that right?"

The girl nods, stepping a little farther away. Her lower lip begins bopping.

Frank goes to the bed and checks the woman. Pulse is fine, breathing even, pupils ... make his gut clench up. He saw it too in the pictures they were shown at the emergency briefing right before they boarded the helicopter. It was from Alan Andersen, who was considered to be Patient Zero at the time, until they found out another person had actually infected him. A person who was still at large, thanks to the inept police. But seeing the dissolving pupils and irises for himself is very different. It's like the woman is going blind. Only the disease is actually making her eyesight better, judging by what they were told about Andersen's case.

"Heightened senses, especially smell and eyesight, but hearing seems improved, too ... physical strength and abilities vastly enhanced ... cognitive processing unaffected or better, though speech becomes harder until gone completely ..."

Frank stares at the woman as pieces of information reverberate through his brain.

She'll wake up any moment, he thinks, swallowing. *Good thing they already tied her down.*

He's not convinced the ropes and the duct tape will hold, though. It didn't seem to have held the person in the other room back. They brought nylon straps for this exact situation. They're in the living room.

He looks at the girl, who's standing off to the side now, hugging herself, shivering in the cold. "Don't you wanna come with me to the living room?" he asks. "You can get a blanket."

The girl shakes her head firmly.

"You don't wanna leave your mother?" Frank guesses. "That's all right." He doesn't want to force her. For one thing, it's not worth the trouble—for another, he may not have the time. "Look, I'm going to get some medical equipment I'll need to make your mother better. If you stay in here with her, don't touch her, okay? It's very important. If you do, you'll fall ill, too. I'll bring you a mask just like mine. It'll protect you. Okay?"

The girl hesitates briefly, then nods. "Okay."

"Good girl." Frank leaves the room and jogs down the hallway.

16

VERONICA

VERONICA TURNS HER HEAD as much as she can, trying to see every window. She's sitting pretty much in the middle of the room, and there are windows on three sides.

"What are you looking for?" the medic asks, turning the coffee table right-side up.

"My father-in-law," Veronica tells him. "He's still out there."

"Flemming?" The doctor places the suitcase on the table and opens it.

"Yeah. He left shortly before you guys arrived."

"You expect him to return?"

"I don't know. Leo did."

The medic gives her a lingering look, then takes out a syringe and unwraps it. He tries to roll up Veronica's left sleeve—which isn't easy because of the strap that's tying down her arm.

"What are you giving me?" she asks.

"I'm not giving you anything," he says, cleaning the crook of her elbow with an ethanol swab. "I'm taking a blood sample for the lab. I assume you're okay with it?"

"Do I have a choice?"

"No. I mean, are you okay with needles?"

"Sure." She looks at him through the visor. He has kind eyes—even though they're worried and right now focused on the task at hand. "There's no antidote yet, then?"

He grunts. "Antidote? You mean a cure? They have no idea what this is yet." He sticks in the needle, and Veronica winces. "Take Covid," he goes on. "The vaccine, how long did it take to develop? Months. Not to mention testing it and rolling it out to the public." He shakes his head and pulls the needle back out. "This thing isn't anything like Covid. And we've only known about it for a few days. I don't think a cure is coming along anytime soon."

She can hear Frank opening doors down the hallway. She checks the windows again, as the doctor carefully puts the syringe away.

"So you have no idea how to treat it?" she asks.

"Not really, no."

"But you called it something, what was it? I mean, you have a name for it."

"They call it Nigrumycosis. But that basically just means 'black fungus.' They don't even really know how to classify it, because it doesn't fit into any of the groups we know of. Honestly, I'm not even sure it's a fungus."

"What do you mean? Why not?"

He shrugs. "At some stages, yes, it acts like a fungus. But in other regards, it presents more like a super-aggressive virus. But don't ask me, I'm not an expert. All I'm saying is, even the experts have no clue yet." He takes out a pill bottle and unscrews the cap. "Open up, please."

Veronica eyes him as he shakes two pills into the cap. "What? I'm still entitled to treatment even though I'm a murderer?"

The doctor shrugs. "You're more than entitled; I'm supposed to force you to take them if you won't do it voluntarily."

"I told you, I don't have the infection."

"How do you know?"

"Because ..." Veronica bites her lip, then decides to tell him. "Because I had it. But it went away. I've been feeling fine ever since."

This gives the doctor pause. "Really?"

"Really. I suspect the same happened to my mother-in-law before she ..." Veronica glances towards the place where Sylvia's remains still lie.

"Well," he says, "you should take the pills anyway. They won't hurt you."

Veronica opens her mouth, and he tips them onto her tongue. She swallows.

"You need something to drink?"

"I'm fine."

He goes through the suitcase again. Veronica checks the windows once more. Still nothing. The darkness is slightly less thick now. She looks at the clock on the wall: 7:50. Normally, she would be having breakfast with Leo by now.

There comes a banging from the hallway. Frank says loudly, "Open the door, girl. Your mom is in there too, right? I know she's sick. I can help her."

"Oh, no," Veronica mutters. "She went into Alice's room ..." She's beginning to feel tense. The situation could very quickly go from bad to worse.

"You shouldn't worry," the doctor tells her, taking out one of those blood pressure measuring devices. "Frank is very cautious."

"He's got no idea what he's up against," Veronica tells him.

The doctor sends her a look, but doesn't answer.

"Have you heard of anyone else like me?" Veronica asks. "Someone else who got it but didn't get sick from it?"

"Yeah. You haven't been following the news?"

"No. Been a little busy. You know, surviving."

He scoffs. "They've found a few dozen people last I heard."

"Well, what happened to them? I mean, are they still fine?"

"As far as I know. But like I said, it's too early to tell anything for sure." He straps the band around Veronica's arm and activates the device. It begins squeezing her. "There's this one guy," he goes on, sounding like he's almost talking to himself. "Ivansen or something. Apparently, he was the first, and he sorta transformed, but then ..." He trails off.

"Then what?" Veronica asks.

Jeppe seems about to answer, when a loud crash from the hallway makes them both jump. The doctor calls out, "Frank, you all right?"

Frank doesn't answer, but a moment later, she hears him say to someone—probably Molly, "It's okay. I'm a doctor. I've come to help."

"Don't hurt her," Veronica mutters, as though Frank could hear her.

The doctor pulls the armband off and instead takes out a scalpel-looking thing and a square piece of clear, hardened plastic. He crouches down next to the armchair. "You said you had it. Did the black rash appear?"

"Yes."

"Where?"

"My hands. My face. A little on my scalp, I think."

"All right. Hold still, please."

"Are you going to cut me?" She tries to pull her hand away as he lowers the knife.

"No, I'm going to scrape off some dead skin from your fingers. It won't hurt if you stay still."

She lets him do it. He goes around her nails, then asks her to turn her hand over, and he scrapes along the furrows in her palm, too. The skin that comes off, he lets drizzle onto the tiny plastic plate

"He's calling you Bille," Veronica remarks, looking at the doctor's eyes. He seems quite handsome under the mask. "That's your last name?"

"Uh-huh."

"I know a Bille. Worked with her for a few years. Stephanie. You know her?"

He raises his eyebrows. "That's my cousin."

"Small world, huh?"

The doctor doesn't answer, but keeps scraping her skin. Despite the awful situation, Veronica can't help but imagine for a brief moment what her life would have been like if she'd settled down with someone like the doctor. Someone smart, educated, committed. Someone she could actually have a conversation with. Have *kids* with. She never really wanted a life like that. She liked to keep the option open, but really, she dreaded the idea of becoming a mom, a homemaker.

Yet suddenly, the thought isn't repulsive at all. Probably because it's no longer an option.

Next life, maybe.

The doctor carefully places it into a small box and clicks the lid shut. "We have a microscope in the helicopter. In a minute, I'll go check if there are any signs of the disease still in your skin. If it's positive, we can't bring you back. You'll have to wait here until they can bring a truck here."

"Oh, you're kidding ..."

"No, I'm sorry. It's the procedure we were told to—"

Footsteps come suddenly from the hallway, and Frank comes into the living room. "Quickly," he says. "Another set of straps."

Jeppe goes to the suitcase, searches briefly, then shakes his head. "I don't think we brought them."

"Of course we did," Frank hisses, coming around the table. He pushes his colleague aside and rummages through the suitcase. He pulls out two straps similar to the ones he's tied Veronica down with. Changing his mind, he puts them back, slams the suitcase and hoists the whole thing with him.

"Okay," Jeppe grunts as Frank leaves the room. "Guess I was finished, then." He still has the skin scrape box in his gloved hand. "I'll go run the test."

"He's not very nice," Veronica remarks, trying to sound sympathetic. She hopes by gaining Jeppe's sympathy, she might get him to release her even if the test turns out positive—she doesn't really think it will, because she's convinced the disease has left her again, but some trace of it might still be left on her skin.

Jeppe hesitates. "He's under a lot of pressure. We all are."

"Yeah, but you can still treat people right."

He scoffs. "I know what you're trying to do."

She sighs. "Please just untie me. I promise I won't run. Even if the test comes back positive."

"Sorry," he says. "It's about national security. Screw that, *international* security." He turns and leaves. A few seconds later, she hears the front door open and close.

Veronica looks at the table. He left the scalpel. It's not within her reach, but if she can move the chair just a few inches ... She leans sideways, but the chair doesn't move. She tries pushing with her feet, and it sorta works, but she moves backwards instead of sideways. Pushing with only one foot, she's able to make the chair turn, but now she has her back to the table.

Veronica is still wrestling with the chair when Frank suddenly cries out: "*No!*" from down the hallway. His voice is full of surprise and fear.

Veronica sits still and listens, her heart pounding. She can hear someone talking in there. It's not Frank. It's also not Molly. It sounds like a grown woman.

Alice. She's awake.

Then, Frank calls out: "*Bille! Need help in here!*" And a few seconds later, this time with real panic in his voice: "*Bille! Jeppe, for God's sake!* **Get in here, now***!*"

Veronica resumes trying to turn the chair, pushing with her feet, twisting her body—when suddenly, a movement catches her eye from the side.

She turns her head towards the east window. Right there, staring in at her through the glass, is Flemming. His eyes bore into hers. A smile tugs at the corner of his mouth. Then he's gone.

Veronica blinks. "Oh, Jesus ... Jeppe! *Jeppe! Come back inside!*"

17

MOLLY

"Molly?"

She jolts at Mom's voice, even though it's only a whisper.

Mom has raised her head slightly—as much as the rope running across her collarbone allows her to—and she's looking at Molly. Her eyes are definitely different, Molly can tell right away; they're not as bad as Leo's, but both the pupil and the blue part around it have faded. At the same time, Mom is smiling, and it looks like her old smile.

"I need your help, sweetie."

Molly shifts her weight from one leg to the other, uncertain what to do or say. "Are you ... are you okay, Mom? I mean ... are you still yourself?"

Mom gives a tiny little laugh. It sounds like how Mom would laugh. "Of course I am. Who else would I be?"

"It's just that ... Uncle Leo, he ... he turned into something ... something completely different."

Mom's expression becomes serious. "I know. It's very sad what happened to him."

Molly wonders briefly how Mom would know about Leo—she's been asleep the whole time—but she doesn't get a chance to ask before Mom goes on.

"I don't want to end up like Uncle Leo. And it's not too late for me."

Molly feels a surge of hope rush through her body and she steps a little closer. "Really? Can the doctors fix you?"

"No, not the doctors. But I can fix myself. If you help me, we can do it together."

Molly tilts her head. "How, Mom?"

Mom is about to answer, when she hears something from the living room. Molly listens. It's the medics, talking together in there. She can hear Veronica say something, too.

"Molly? Look at me, sweetie."

Molly looks at Mom. She seems a bit more serious now.

"The only thing you need to do is to give me the box cutter your grandma left in the drawer right there." She gestures with her head towards the nightstand. "That's all."

Molly frowns. "Are you ... are you going to hurt the doctors, Mom?"

Mom grins, and this time, Molly can tell her mouth is a bit too wide. Her teeth look different, too. There's too much space between them, and they look thin and pointy, like tiny icebergs protruding from the gums.

"Of course not, sweetie. What do you think I am? A monster? I'm just going to cut the tape so I can get up from here. I can't do much to help myself as long as I'm tied down like this, can I?"

"But ... I don't understand," Molly says, hesitating. "How can you fix yourself? Shouldn't we rather—"

"Look, missy," Mom says, snapping into her strict voice. "I don't need to explain myself to you. You do as I tell you, or you won't have me around for much longer. You get that? In ten seconds, the doctor will return, and it'll be too late. He's going to strap me down even harder, and I'll never get free. He's not here to fix me—don't believe their lies, Molly.

They're going to prod and probe me and run all kinds of nasty experiments on me."

Molly's heart is beating fast. She's torn. On the one hand, she wants to believe Mom—wants to badly. But on the other hand, she can't shake the awful memory of her uncle Leo and what he tried to do to her. But Mom isn't really that changed yet. She can still talk and everything. It's just her eyes and teeth. Maybe she's not—

"Molly!" Mom hisses. "Snap out of it and give me the box cutter! He's coming."

Mom's right. Molly can hear footsteps coming down the hallway. She rushes to the nightstand, opens the drawer, and sees an empty roll of tape and a lime-green box cutter. She grabs the box cutter and closes the drawer just as the medic appears in the doorway. Molly turns around and hides the box cutter behind her back.

The doctor is hoisting along a big suitcase, the gun still hanging on his back. As he sees Molly, he pauses briefly, and for an awful moment, Molly is sure he sees right through her and notices the box cutter in her hand. But all he says is, "Don't stand so close to the bed, Molly."

Molly staggers sideways, going to the foot of the bed, making sure to keep her front to the doctor. It must look awfully suspicious, but the doctor doesn't seem to notice. He puts the suitcase on the floor, opens it, and begins rummaging through the contents.

He glances up at her. "You didn't touch your mother, did you, Molly?"

Molly shakes her head. She looks guiltily at Mom, but her eyes are closed again. She's pretending to sleep.

The doctor pulls out two long, yellow, belt-looking things with clasps at the ends and approaches the bed.

Molly hears Mom's voice in her mind: "*He's going to strap me down even harder, and I'll never get free.*"

"What ... what are those for?" Molly asks.

"It's just an extra precaution," the doctor says, fastening one of the clasps to the bed frame. Then he runs it around Mom's wrist and pulls it tight. The strap looks very strong. Not even a bodybuilder could rip it, and certainly not Mom.

Molly feels a stab of regret. She should have listened to Mom. The doctor isn't here to help her. If he was, why wouldn't he free her instead of tying her down even more? In a flash, Molly sees them lifting the bed with the helicopter, flying Mom to the mainland, placing her in some lab, and then running painful experiments on her, just like they do with rats and mice.

Molly's heart is beating hard below her chin now. She moves to the other side of the bed while the doctor is securing the first strap. A movement catches her eye. Mom's hand—the one on this side, the one that's still not strapped down—is beckoning her closer. Mom's eyes are still closed, but the gesture is unmistakable.

The doctor takes the other strap and comes around the bed. "Step away, Molly. I already told you: You're standing too close."

Molly makes a snap decision. It's now or never. She uses her thumb to push out the box cutter's blade, and then she starts cutting the tape that's holding Mom's arm.

"Whoa, whoa! No, stop, what are you doing?" the doctor exclaims, rushing to reach Molly. His hip bumps into the corner of the bed, and that's probably what makes the difference. It slows him down just long enough that Molly can cut the last tape. But there's still the rope, and there's no way she can cut that. Turns out, she doesn't need to. The doctor reaches her, grabs her wrist and pulls her away hard. "Are you out of your damn mind, child? I told you, she's dang—"

Mom groans, and there's a crisp snap as she raises her arm and the nylon rope gives way. She immediately grabs the doctor's suit and rips through it with her nails, leaving a big hole right on his belly. The doctor cries out, staggers back and fumbles with his suit, trying desperately to pull the hole shut. But too much fabric is missing, and he decides instead to lunge forward and try to secure Mom's arm with the last strap.

He quickly regrets that decision.

Even with only one arm free, Mom is clearly much stronger than the doctor. He grabs her forearm with both hands, but she tears free with a hard tug, pulling him closer at the same time. She grabs for his head and tears off the mask.

"No!" he cries out, trying to pull away once more. But this time, Mom is too fast. She slaps him across the face.

It's not even that hard. As though she didn't really try to hurt him.

The doctor stumbles, almost falls over. His gloved hand goes to his cheek and touches it. His eyes are big and shocked. His hair sweaty and in disarray. He's not as old as Molly thought, not much older than Mom.

"You ... you touched me," he mutters.

Mom isn't listening. She's busy ripping and tearing through the tape holding her down with her nails. In a matter of seconds, she's able to sit up. Her eyes meet Molly's. Mom's expression is wild. She breathes fast, and she smiles at Molly, and this time, the smile isn't at all like her mom's. It's way too wide, way too hungry, and Molly gets the clear sense that Mom made an effort before to hide her new, altered features. But now, she doesn't need to pretend anymore.

"Thanks, sweetie," she says. "I owe you one."

The doctor comes rushing past Molly. He bumps into her and almost knocks her over. He runs to the suitcase, falls to his knees, and pulls out a bottle of something. Unscrewing the cap, he slathers a clear liquid on his cheek and rubs it in hard.

"Bille!" he cries out. "Need help in here!"

Mom rips the last tape and rope holding her legs, and then she stands up.

"Bille!" the doctor shouts, getting to his feet as he sees Mom standing. "Jeppe, for God's sake! *Get in here, now*!" He pulls the gun over his head and puts it against his shoulder.

Mom gives off a hiss, spins around on her heel, and dives headfirst through the window, slamming it open all the way before she disappears into the darkness.

"Fuck!" the doctor spits, running back around the bed. He points the gun out into the cold morning air, panning it this way then that, but he can't seem to see Mom out there, because he soon pulls the gun back inside and says again: "Fuck!" Then he notices Molly standing there, and he glares at her. "You know what you have done?" Not waiting for an answer, he strides towards the door. "Bille! Where the hell are you?"

18

VERONICA

SOMEONE COMES RUNNING INTO the room.

Veronica really hopes to see Jeppe, but instead, she sees Frank. And to make it worse, his mask is missing, revealing a gray beard and wild eyes.

He's holding the gun in one hand as he looks around. "Jeppe? For chrissake, where are you, man?" His gaze lands on Veronica, and he snarls, "What did you do to him?"

"He went outside," Veronica tells him, nodding towards the north side of the cabin.

Frank turns to leave.

"Wait!" Veronica calls out, causing him to pause briefly and look back. "I just saw my father-in-law. If you go out there, keep the gun ready."

Frank wrinkles his nose, as though taking advice from her is disgusting to him. But he nonetheless shoulders the shotgun before he runs on down the hallway.

She hears the front door being ripped open.

Then the house falls quiet.

Veronica considers calling out to Molly, but she's not sure it's wise. If Alice has gotten free, she might be looking for the girl. If Molly has managed to hide somewhere, Veronica doesn't want the girl to hear her call for her and cause her to reveal her hiding place.

Besides, Veronica is a sitting duck herself, so attracting Alice's attention would be a very bad idea.

She resumes working the chair, trying to turn it around. It's not easy, but she makes slow headway. Her hand steadily comes closer to the place where the scalpel is. If she can get it just a little closer, she might be able to bump into the table and cause the scalpel to drop into her hand. Even with the straps in place, she can still turn her palm up just enough to catch it. She'll probably cut herself, but that's a risk she needs to take.

A low rumble from outside. At first, Veronica takes it to be a second helicopter approaching—the cops finally showing up as promised—but then the lights come on outside, and she realizes it's the medic chopper starting up.

"Are they leaving?" she blurts out, straining to see through the windows. She can't actually see the aircraft, but snow is being whipped up and flung against the house as the rotors pick up speed. "No, you can't just go!" Veronica cries out, even though there's no chance they'll hear her. "Damnit..."

She bites down and works harder to position the chair.

It takes her another few minutes, but she actually manages to get it turned and moved into just the right spot. She keeps her hand open and begins rocking from side to side as much as the strap allows her. It's not really enough to get the chair to bump against the table, at least not hard enough to move the scalpel.

"Fucking *damnit*!" she hisses, out of breath from the exertion. Her thighs and calves are burning, her back is aching.

The helicopter sounds like it's almost at full throttle now, ready to take off. Veronica blinks several times, thinking hard. She looks at her legs. They're not strapped down.

Maybe she can get one of them onto the table and push the scalpel into her hand? No, that won't work. She can't twist her body like that. She can push the scalpel onto the floor, but what good will it do her there?

She seriously considers calling for Molly, when someone comes running into the room.

Veronica cries out in shock, expecting to see Alice or Flemming.

To her surprise, it's Jeppe. He's brought the shotgun, and he's still wearing his suit, which looks intact.

"What the hell are you guys doing?" Veronica shouts over the roar of the chopper. "Are you just leaving?"

Jeppe comes to her, places the gun on the table, and crouches down. "I'm sorry. Frank has been exposed. We have to get him—"

"So you're just running away like a couple of cowards?" Veronica spits.

He looks up at her through the visor. "Frank wanted to leave you here for the cops, but I insisted on going back in and freeing you."

"That's very noble of you," Veronica snarls as he begins fumbling with the buckle for the chest strap. "But I'm not coming with you, not unless we also bring Molly."

Jeppe pauses to look at her again. "I'm sorry, but neither of you are coming. I just didn't want you to be stuck here for hours."

Veronica frowns. "What?"

He shrugs. "The cops should have been here by now. Perhaps something happened. Perhaps they had to abort. Frank tried reaching them over the radio, but he couldn't—"

"So you really are just leaving us here? Me, and the little girl?"

He shakes his head and resumes tugging at the buckle. "I'm really sorry."

"Yeah, you should be," Veronica tells him, and she's about to say something else, when out of nowhere, a huge frame rises up behind Jeppe.

Flemming's moustache is gone.

The size of her father-in-law makes it all the more shocking that he somehow managed to get so close without Veronica noticing. Flemming towers over the doctor, his eyes almost completely blank, and Veronica screams as he goes for the mask. Jeppe reacts with incredible speed, turning halfway around and raising his arms. Flemming doesn't get a proper grip of the mask and instead begins grappling with the doctor.

"*The gun!*" Veronica screams. "*Shoot him!*"

Jeppe tries to go for the weapon, but Flemming is clearly both faster and stronger. He grabs his wrist and with a violent yank, he tears off the glove and rips the sleeve like it was made of paper. Jeppe roars and tries to pull his hand away, but it's too late. Flemming grabs it with his other hand—the size different makes it look like a parent grabbing a kid who doesn't want to follow along. Flemming lets go immediately, and Jeppe pulls his hand to his chest.

For a split-second, they just stare at each other, as all three of them realize what just happened.

Then Jeppe goes for the gun. He manages to get his hands on it, and as he swings it around to take aim, Flemming slaps the barrel hard enough for the shotgun to go flying across the room.

Once more, the two men—if Flemming can still be called that—stare at each other for a moment.

"Please," Veronica hears Jeppe say. "Please don't hurt me …"

Flemming points over his shoulder and utters a single word, "Leave."

Jeppe—clearly not believing that he's really allowed to go—hesitates. Which makes Flemming bare his teeth and step forward. Jeppe jolts, skids sideways, then runs for the hallway, clutching his hand.

"Don't go!" Veronica screams. "Don't go to the mainland!"

Jeppe is already gone.

Veronica looks up at Flemming. He takes a few steps closer. Clearly not as transformed as his son, Flemming still moving mostly like Flemming. But Veronica can tell his movements already have a trace of that insect-like character. He stops in front of the chair, towering over her, breathing, and his tongue touches the corner of his mouth—a habit he evidently didn't kick yet.

He says something Veronica can't hear because of the roar of the helicopter which has grown even louder. But she doesn't need to hear it. She can read his lips.

"Veronica."

"You can't infect me," Veronica says, hoping she sounds more defiant than she feels. "I already had it. I kicked it. I'm immune."

Flemming just smiles. The smile makes Veronica realize she's about to die.

She thought she was ready. Thought she'd gotten used to knowing that death was not far away. But apparently, her system isn't ready to give up without a fight. Because red-hot panic explodes from her solar plexus and floods her entire system, gearing up to do whatever she can to keep Flemming from eating her alive.

There are no weapons within reach. The shotgun landed somewhere over by the kitchen area, and the scalpel is no longer on the table. Apparently, it fell to the floor when Jeppe grabbed the gun.

She's hopelessly trapped. Her arms pinned to the chair, her torso only able to move a little, but not enough to stand up. The only thing she can move is her legs. She kicks Flemming hard in the groin. The instep connects perfectly. Flemming hardly seems bothered. Veronica kicks again, aiming for his shin. He moves his leg away. Veronica pushes both her boots hard into the floor, causing the armchair to flip back. She's not sure what the plan is—maybe getting on her back will cause the torso strap to loosen, maybe her hand will end up close enough to the scalpel, maybe—

Flemming stops the chair from tilting by placing a hand on the armrest.

Veronica tries to kick him again, but he moves to the side and out of her reach. All she can do is glare up at him. "Don't do it. I'm warning you!"

As she says it, she realizes she can hear the words much better—the sound of the helicopter has quickly grown faint. And along with it her only hope for help.

Flemming crouches down and grabs her thigh with both hands, pinning it in place. His grip is incredibly hard, and Veronica can't help but give off a yelp of pain.

Flemming glances at her one last time. He smiles as he tells her, "Always loved those runner's legs."

"No," Veronica hears herself say. "No, no, don't! *Nooo!*"

Flemming bends over, opens his mouth and bites off a chunk of Veronica's thigh.

19

MOLLY

SHE DOESN'T WANT TO stay in Mom's bedroom, but she also doesn't want to leave.

After the doctor leaves, Molly just stands there for what feels like several minutes, looking from the door to the window. She expects someone to come back into the room from either direction any second. But it doesn't happen.

Then she suddenly hears the sound of the helicopter again. It sounds like it's starting up.

Molly gasps and runs to the door. She glances down the hallway. She can see some of the living room from here, but it doesn't seem like anybody's in there. She runs to her own room and goes to the window. The lights from the helicopter are very bright, and snow is being whirled around in the air, so Molly can't really see anything.

"Are they leaving?" she whispers, her breath fogging the glass. "Did Veronica forget about me?"

She considers opening the window and calling for them, but they probably won't hear her over the engine. If she wants to go along with them, she needs to go out there.

So, she turns around and heads for the door.

Just before she reaches it, Grandpa steps into view.

Molly stops dead in her tracks, a scream lodging itself in her throat. Grandpa sees her and stops too. He looks at her, and Molly wants to scream again, but she can't. The sight of Grandpa is in some ways worse than Leo, because she can still mostly see Grandpa. Yet his face is changed, his arms and fingers too long, his frame a little wrong. But as they stare at each other in the dim light, she could swear there's kindness in his eyes for a moment.

Then it goes away—not completely; it's still there, but now it's overshadowed by something else. Something foreign. Something hungry.

"Grandpa," Molly croaks. "Please don't hurt me."

Grandpa cocks his head, and he says in a voice that Molly can just make out over the helicopter, "Would never hurt you, cupcake."

"But, Grandpa—"

He raises his hand and places a thin index finger over his lips. Then he blinks twice, just like he always did whenever they shared a secret, and he reaches in and gently closes the door.

Once again, Molly just stands there, not sure what to do. Grandpa clearly didn't want her to follow. He wanted her to stay in here. He said he wouldn't hurt her, but Molly isn't sure he will—or can—keep that promise if she disobeys him.

She goes to the bed and sees her phone on the nightstand. She texts Veronica: *You leaving? I'm still in my room.*

She's not sure Veronica will see the message. A few minutes pass by, but no reply comes in.

Then the helicopter suddenly takes off. The light rises up into the sky, and the noise from the engine becomes less deafening. Within just a minute or so, Molly can hear her own breathing again.

She's in two minds about what to do. Stay in the room or go look who's left in the house. She finds it very strange that

Veronica would leave without her. It's much more likely that either she's hurt—or worse, dead—or she's still here.

As though to answer her thoughts, she suddenly hears Veronica's voice from the living room: "*Don't do it. I'm warning you.*"

There's fear in her voice. And anger.

Clearly, someone is about to do something Veronica doesn't care for. But who? One of the doctors? Grandpa? Mom?

Hearing Veronica's voice, even though she's obviously in a bad situation, has filled Molly with hope. At least she's not alone. Veronica didn't leave her.

She hears Veronica again—this time, she gives off a tiny little scream. Sorta like the noise you make when you bang your toe.

Molly bites her lip. *Maybe she needs my help?*

Molly isn't sure what she can do to help Veronica, but one thing's for sure: Sitting around in here isn't doing her any good.

So, Molly goes to the door, opens it, and glances out into the hallway. She hears Grandpa's voice from the living room. He talks pretty low, so Molly can't make out the words.

She slips along the wall, edging closer to the living room. More and more of the room comes into view, and Molly almost freezes as she sees Grandpa. Even though he's kneeling, he's very big. Next to him is the armchair that Grandma used to sit in, and in the chair is Veronica. It takes Molly a moment to realize that Veronica is strapped to the chair and unable to get up.

Grandpa is holding one of Veronica's legs, and as he bends over, Veronica shouts: "No. No, no, don't! *Nooo!*"

Then—to Molly's horror—Grandpa digs his teeth into Veronica's thigh. Her scream turns piercing as Grandpa pulls his head back up. Even from this angle, with Grandpa facing mostly away from her, Molly can see a flap of skin disappear into his mouth as he chews it greedily.

Molly feels dizzy. The room moves like it did on the ferry on the way over. She blinks to try and make it stop, and she almost loses her balance. Taking a steadying step, her foot hits something. She looks down dreamily, and at the sight of the object on the floor, the dizziness subsides a little.

A single, clear thought makes it into her head.

Huh. Maybe it's not too late.

20

VERONICA

THE PAIN IS DEFINITELY the worst she's ever felt.

Way worse than when she sprained her ankle. Or when she burned herself with piping hot tea water.

She's heard from friends that childbirth is the most painful thing a woman can experience. If it's worse than this, then Veronica is happy she never had kids.

She screams as loudly as she can, the sound filling her ears, then tuning out. She realizes she's about to pass out, but a new wave of pain brings her back again, and the sound returns as she realizes she's still screaming.

She manages to look and through a tunnel she sees Flemming's face next to her, his cheeks bulging as he's munching away on a mouth of Veronica's skin and flesh. She looks down, her narrow field of vision landing on her thigh, and she sees a gaping crater. It's filling up with blood and quickly begins spilling over.

I'm getting eaten alive, Veronica realizes, and she almost wants to pass out for real. She doesn't want to be around for this. But her mind won't let go. Still clinging to life with no hope of anything left but excruciating pain, she finds herself still looking around for a solution, for a way out.

But there is none.

She hears Flemming make a wet noise as he tilts back his head and forces the bite down his gullet. She can actually see it go down. He looks at her, a trickle of blood runs from his lips as he smiles, and then he bends over for another bite.

"No," Veronica croaks. "Stop."

But he doesn't stop.

Veronica wants to headbutt him as he bends over, but she can't reach. She notices peripherally that he's no longer holding on to her leg that tightly, so she lifts it, using it to press his head upward, and then she flings her own head forward.

Their skulls connect with a painful clash. Veronica's forehead hits Flemming right on the temple. She hardly feels it; the pain from the bite wound blocks out every other sensation. Flemming seems to feel it, though. He turns his head to glare at Veronica. He doesn't exactly look like he's in pain, but he's definitely angry.

"Fuck you," Veronica hisses, thinking to herself: *Maybe I can at least get him to end it quickly.* "Fuck you and your stuck-up wife and your loser son. I'm glad they're both dead."

Flemming's face goes through a surprisingly human range of emotions. His expression turns from shock to sorrow to rage. His lips quiver as he pulls them back, revealing all his blood-smeared teeth—a few of them are still human, but most of them have been replaced with pointy catlike fangs. "I'll tear you apart piece by piece," he growls.

"Go ahead, you fat piece of—"

And then …

Then, out of nowhere, Molly is standing there, right behind him.

Veronica stares at the girl, almost certain she's seeing an illusion. Some wild fata morgana conjured up by her desperate mind as one last attempt at solace.

But the tears streaming down her face look very much real. So does the shotgun in the girl's shaking hands.

Flemming sees Veronica staring at something, so he turns his head.

Just as he does, Molly cries out shrilly: "*I'm sorry, Grandpa!*"

There's a flash and a very loud bang.

21

MOLLY

SHE'S NOT SURE SHE'S holding it right—she's probably not. She's also not sure that "the safety's off"—she doesn't even know what that means, exactly, but she's heard the phrase in the movies. She doesn't even know if there are bullets—or whatever they're called—in the gun.

All she knows for sure is where the trigger is.

And she squeezes it as hard as she can.

She aims for Grandpa's back, right between the shoulder blades. But because he turns his head just at the last second, the shot seems to go for his ribs instead.

Whatever the case, Molly doesn't find out right away. Because the moment she pulls the trigger, the gun is suddenly yanked back with incredible force, dragging Molly along with it. It's ripped from her hands, and she falls on her butt. There's also a sound, but it was so loud, Molly didn't really hear it. There's just a pop in her ears, and then no more sounds.

She sits up, feeling pain in her hands and arms from the violent pull of the gun. She looks around, trying to see whoever snuck up behind her and yanked the weapon from her. But no one's around. And the gun is just lying on the floor, smoke coming from the muzzle.

I definitely fired it, she thinks. *But why did it knock me over?*

The only answer she can think of is that firing the gun must have been what did it. There's a word she's heard somewhere, flickering at the edge of her mind: recoil. She's not completely sure what it means, and it doesn't really matter now.

She turns her head to look at Grandpa. He's keeled over, one hand on the floor, the other clutching his side. His hand is covering what looks like a big hole in his shirt. Dark blood is seeping out between his fingers. He coughs, and more blood comes spraying out of his mouth.

It's an awful sight, seeing Grandpa hurt like this, and Molly begins crying again. She can't actually hear her own sobs, but she feels the tears.

Then she notices a movement behind Grandpa. It's Veronica. She's thrashing her head back and forth, her black hair whipping around her head. She's staring at Molly and seemingly shouting something. The weird head movement is apparently meant to catch Molly's attention—Veronica is still tied down and can't wave or in any other way signal with her hands—because as soon as Molly looks at her, she stops moving but keeps staring at her and shouting. She's repeating a single word: Again! Again!

Molly realizes with a sinking feeling that Veronica wants her to shoot Grandpa one more time.

She looks at him. He stops coughing, wipes his mouth in his sleeve, then turns his head towards her. Molly has seen Grandpa angry a few times, but never with her. Now, he's staring at her with so much hate, it makes her skin icy all over. He's not just about to reprimand her—he's going to kill her. Molly is sure of it. So when he lunges for her, she kicks herself backwards out of his reach. He slips in his own blood and collapses onto his belly.

Molly jumps to her feet and runs around him. She doesn't even consider going for the gun—there's no way she's firing it again. Instead, she runs to Veronica. Her hearing is somewhat returned, and she can hear her own weeping voice: "I can't do it, Veronica! I can't! I can't do it, I'm sorry!"

Veronica stares at her and then lowers her head quickly. Stares at her, then lowers her head. It's like she's pointing down with her eyes.

"What ... what is it?" Molly asks, looking at her feet. She wipes away the tears and sees a weird, thin-bladed knife lying there.

"Take it!" Veronica shouts, her voice just penetrating the buzzing sound in Molly's ears. "Cut me free, Molly!"

And Molly finally gets it.

She bends down, takes the knife, and just as she's about to cut the strap pinning Veronica's arm to the chair, Veronica screams: "Watch out!"

Molly looks up to see Grandpa coming for her. He's on his feet, but hunched over, his hand still holding the gunshot wound. The other one is reaching out for Molly. His face is pale, but his expression determined. Molly shrieks and tries to back up, but she bumps into the coffee table.

Veronica kicks hard with her good leg and hits Grandpa right below the knee. He cries out, loses his balance and falls over once again.

Veronica stares at Molly. "Cut it. Cut it now, Molly. Hurry!"

Molly looks down at her hand, not sure if the knife is still there. It is. She places the blade on the strap and begins sawing.

"Harder!" Veronica urges her. "Push harder. Never mind if you cut me."

Molly increases the pressure, and the blade slides halfway through the strap.

Grandpa pops back up and grabs Molly's arm just as the strap is cut. She screams and tries to pull free, but he's too strong, and he's pulling her towards him, growling.

Veronica yanks the knife from Molly's hand and thrusts it into Grandpa's face. Grandpa roars out and lets go of Molly.

Veronica pulls the knife back, and Molly doesn't want to see Grandpa's face, but she can't help catch a glimpse of his punctured eye before he slaps his palm over it. His other eye closes briefly, then opens again and fixes on Veronica. He's about to attack her, but Veronica has used the few seconds to cut the other two straps, and she's now free. She swats at Grandpa with the knife again, but this time he manages to pull his face back. Veronica jumps out of the chair and runs.

For an awful moment, Molly thinks she's leaving. That she'll simply bolt and leave Molly alone with Grandpa.

But then she sees Veronica pick up the gun. Grandpa must have guessed her intentions, because he's gotten to his feet and is stumbling towards her, both arms outstretched.

He's only a few feet away when Veronica fires the gun.

Molly sees Grandpa's head change shape. She sees a cascade of something flying from it. And she sees him collapse to the floor.

Then she sees no more.

22

VERONICA

AS SOON AS SHE'S made sure Flemming isn't getting back up—he's definitely not; he took the shot right to the face, and half his skull is missing—she clicks the sling free from the gun and wraps it around her thigh a few inches above the wound. She pulls it tight and ties it as hard as she can.

Satisfied it's not coming off, she limps to the girl. The pain in her thigh has been transformed into mostly numbness. It feels like her leg is simply not there. Which must have something to do with blood loss—she's been bleeding like a punctured water bag. Now, with the sling in place, it seems to have been reduced to a slow trickle.

Molly has fainted next to the armchair. Veronica checks that she's breathing and that she's not hurt.

Leaving the girl, Veronica jumps on one leg down the hallway. In Alice's bedroom, she finds what she's looking for: the medic's suitcase. Staring down into a wide arrangement of equipment, Veronica sees a bottle marked "Antiseptic Solution." She grabs it and pours the liquid straight into the wound. It burns like crazy, sending flames all the way up to her hip and down into her toes. Veronica screams out and almost loses consciousness. Blinking hard, she drops the bottle and takes instead a clear bag full of cotton balls. She rips open the bag with her teeth, pulls up her pant leg—luckily, they're very stretchable—and smooshes a handful of the cotton into the wound, producing another wave of fiery pain. Then she takes a roll of gauze and begins wrapping her leg, pinning the cotton in place.

She's breathing fast as she watches her hands work. The gauze goes round and round, gradually covering the wound. She makes sure to tighten it as much as she can, and she feels the pressure from the cotton. There's a lot of blood—her pants and skin are both soaked in it—but not as much as she feared. Veronica knows little about anatomy, but she knows the femoral vein is one of the biggest, and if that's cut open, you're pretty much dead meat. Apparently, Flemming didn't bite her deep enough to reach it.

When she's done, the bleeding seems to have stopped completely.

Veronica lies down on the bed, breathes deeply, and begins drifting off. She's never been this tired in her life. Not even after a marathon.

Just before she goes, she thinks: *I'm still alive.*

She falls asleep with a smile.

23

TIM

Pulling over, Tim parks the car.

It's dark outside. The headlights are off—Tim no longer needs the lights to see—so he's pretty certain the soldiers up ahead haven't noticed them approaching. They're still more than a mile away, yet Tim can make out the barrier clearly.

"What is it?" Helena asks, yawning as she wakes from her slumber.

"They sealed off the city," Tim says. "We can't use any of the roads."

"But your cabin," Helena says, turning her head to see the hill behind them. "Isn't it back there?"

"Yeah. But Buddy is at Alan's. At least I hope he's still there." That last part, Tim murmurs under his breath.

"So … how do we get to him?"

Tim takes a deep breath. "I think it might be best if I go alone. Like I said, I can't drive into town, so I'll need to go on foot."

"Do I just wait here for you, then?"

"No," Tim says, looking around. It's mostly frozen fields out here with a few houses scattered about. "I wouldn't feel safe with you sitting out here. I'll drive you to the cabin. You wait in the basement, and then I'll go fetch Buddy."

"Okay, but, Dad ... don't you think the police might be waiting up there for you?"

He looks at her. "Why?"

She gestures to the dashboard. "Well, you heard what they said on the radio earlier. After that woman posted the video on Facebook, you're kinda world famous. And it sounded like you're also wanted."

Tim grunts. "They have no idea where I am. They've got no way of tracking me."

"But they've got your address."

"No, they haven't."

"Dad, please. They said your full name. Of course they also know where you live."

"No," Tim says, tapping his temple. "They *think* they know where I live."

Helena frowns. "What's that supposed to mean?"

Tim begins turning the car around.

"Dad?" she asks, eyeing him intently. "What have you done?"

"Remember when we moved out to the cabin?"

"No, I don't. I was, like, three."

"Yeah. I tried getting it approved as an all-year residence, but they wouldn't let me. I mean, it's perfectly livable. Running water, heating system, no mold or anything. Your mom really liked the place, so ... I had a friend help me out."

Helena is still burning him. "Help you out ... how?"

Tim shrugs. "Officially, we never moved to the cabin. According to the Civil Registration Office, I still live on Parkvej 10."

Helena is quiet. Then she scoffs. "Seriously? And you don't think anyone's ever found out the house is empty?"

"No. I have an old car parked there. I go there a few times a year, cut the lawn, pick up mail, empty the gutters. And I installed one of those systems that'll randomly switch lights on and off. You know, for when you go on a holiday?"

"Jesus Christ, Dad. Are you serious right now?"

"Yeah."

She bursts out laughing. "You're like one of those doomsday preppers! Why would you go through all this trouble?"

"I just don't like being on the grid." Tim sends her a crooked smile. "Guess that paranoia is finally paying off, huh? We have a perfectly fine hiding place and no one even knows the place exists. I had my guy fix it so that it looks like the cabin was torn down years ago. The road leading up there isn't even on any GPS maps."

Helena does her best not to smile. "You're crazy, you know that?"

"Never claimed otherwise."

She's quiet for a moment. "But listen, Dad. Since we're confessing about illegal stuff … I can drive up there myself, you know."

He looks at her. "You can?"

"Yeah. I can drive."

"Since when?"

"Since Freddie taught me."

Tim slows down the car and looks at her. "Are you sure? It could be icy. And the road up there—"

"I know the road like the back of my hand. I'll be careful." She unbuckles. "You go get Buddy and you guys meet me up there. I'll get the place heated up."

She's about to open her door. Tim stops her with a hand on her thigh. "Hold on, honey."

"Dad, it's fine. Really."

"No, just hear me out. There's a basement under the cabin. I know you don't know about it, but it's—"

"I know about it," Helena confesses.

It's Tim's turn to frown now. "You do?"

"Yeah. I mean, I've never been down there. But the hatch is under the rug in the scullery, right?"

"Yeah ..."

Helena shrugs. "I found it one day I was playing. I couldn't get it open—there was a big padlock on it. I figured it was just where you kept your guns?"

"It is. But there's a bed down there, too. And canned foods and water enough for six months. It's very safe. I want you to hide down there until I come. Just in case ... someone shows up."

Helena seems to get it, and Tim's glad he doesn't need to elaborate. "Do you have a key?"

"It's a combination. The code is 2407."

Helena smiles. "My birthday."

"Yeah."

"Okay, got it."

Without further discussion, she gets out and walks around the car.

Tim just watches her. He's struck by how much she reminds him of Anya.

You'd be proud of her, honey.

He pulls the handbrake and takes off his seat belt.

24

VERONICA

IT'S THE COLD THAT brings her back.

She's shivering violently.

Opening her eyes, she groans and looks around a room she doesn't immediately recognize. Greyish daylight is coming in through a single window. Veronica is splayed out on a bed. It feels like she's been gone for days. The sleep was so deep, it takes her memory several seconds to recall the events that led her here.

"Molly," she croaks, sitting up with a jerk.

The movement sparks a blistering firework of pain from her leg. Grinding her teeth, she sees the gauze and in a flash, she remembers all too vividly the feeling of Flemming's teeth slicing through her flesh.

"Oh, jeez, that really happened …"

As the pain little by little subsides and turns into a dull, warm throbbing, she checks the bandage a little closer—which isn't easy, because her fingers are all stiff and quivering. It doesn't look very professional, but evidently she did an all right job, because the bleeding has stopped. The compression is still in place, and that probably saved her life. Maybe it also helped that her entire circulation seems to have slowed down to a crawl, leaving her ice cold.

She finally becomes aware of a faint rumble in the distance. She recognizes it. A helicopter is approaching. Still far away, it could be headed for this cabin, or someplace else.

Veronica gets out of bed, carefully testing her bad leg. As soon as she's vertical, the pain increases. She tries to jump on the good leg, but she immediately loses balance and has to sit back down on the bed. The bad leg hurts like hell, especially if she tries to extend it.

Well, my running days are over, that's for sure.

She looks around for anything she can use as a crutch. Her best option is the floor lamp. It's one of those retro kinds with a wooden pole and wide base and a shade made of fabric. Scooching sideways, she yanks the cord from the wall and wraps it around the pole so it won't get entangled in her feet. Then she takes off the shade and unscrews the bulb. Standing up, she places the top of the pole inside her armpit. It works surprisingly well. The lamp is a bit heavier than she would have liked, but it's great for support. Now that she's able to walk—or rather, limp—she leaves the room and is pleased to find that the hallway is somewhat warmer.

She makes her way to the living room, which is a little warmer still. The skin on her face and hands begins to prickle. Flemming is lying exactly where she left him, the shotgun too. She sees Molly's legs behind the armchair and goes to her. She's breathing calmly as though simply sleeping.

Veronica considers letting her sleep, but then she notices the sound of the helicopter has grown louder.

She limps to the window and looks out. The sky is overcast, and there's a thick, white mist in the air, making it hard to see very far. She can't make out the aircraft. But it's very likely that it's headed for them.

Thank God. Finally.

Veronica goes to the kitchen, opens the hot tap and drinks greedily. Filling her belly with warm water makes her hungry. She opens the fridge and grabs half a sandwich that Alice didn't finish yesterday. Chowing it down in a couple of minutes, she feels a little more energized. She goes to wake up Molly, but finds her gone.

Veronica blinks. "What the ...? Molly? Molly!"

"Yes?"

Veronica spins around so fast she almost loses her balance.

Molly comes in from the hallway and sends her a beaming smile.

"There you are! I thought you ... never mind. I'm so glad to see you!"

Molly rushes to her, embracing her.

"Whoa, easy, sweetie," Veronica says, but she can't help but smile. "Are you okay? Are you hurt?"

"No," Molly says, looking up at her. Her smile turns sad and her eyes fill up with tears. "Is it real? I mean ... did it all really happen?"

Veronica sighs and looks around the living room. "Yeah, I'm afraid it did."

Molly begins sobbing. "I went to find Mom but I couldn't ... I thought maybe it was all just a dream ..."

"Wish it was," Veronica says, rubbing the girl's back while clutching the lamp. "Listen, Molly. The police are coming. Can you hear them?"

Molly lifts her head, sniffs and listens. Then she nods.

"They'll take care of you. They'll probably send us both to a hospital to get us checked out. They just want to make sure we're not carrying the infection."

Molly's face stiffens at this. "What will they do to us?"

"Nothing, don't worry. They'll just take a blood sample and stuff. Once they find out we—"

"No, I mean, what will they do if we are infected?"

"Well, we're not," Veronica smiles. "I'm immune, and none of them touched your skin, so you're fine, too."

Molly eyes her. There's real concern in her eyes.

For some reason, Veronica's heart is beating faster. "Listen, sweetie," she tells the girl, taking her shoulder. "You're not sick, okay? If you caught it, you'd have …"

Veronica stops talking as Molly raises her hand.

The black stuff is covering the soft part of her thumb where the prints are. It's snaking down to her palm, filling the creases and reaching for the other fingers.

"Oh," Veronica says—as though Molly just informed her they're out of milk. She can't think of anything else to say.

"I tried to wash it off," Molly confesses, looking at her palm. "Just now. I couldn't." She looks up at Veronica with a guilty expression. "It must've been when I touched Mom's eyelid. I know I shouldn't've but I didn't think about it when it happened … it was just for half a second or so."

Suddenly, the sound of the helicopter is very loud in Veronica's ears.

"It's okay," she hears herself say. "You, uhm … you'll be fine, I'm sure. You're probably immune. Just like me."

Molly closes her hand and presses it gently against her chest. "What will they do to me, Veronica?"

Veronica swallows. "They'll probably … they'll probably, uhm …"

She can't lie to the girl. She just can't.

So, she makes a decision.

Grabbing the girl's shoulder again, she squeezes it hard. "Listen, Molly. We need to get out of here."

25

VERONICA

"Are you sure you can drive it?" Molly asks, looking doubtful at Veronica as she fixes the lamp pole to the side of the idling scooter. "I mean, with your bad leg. Maybe it's better if we—"

"It's fine," Veronica says, biting back the pain. "As long as I can keep it extended, it doesn't really hurt. Come on, now. Climb onboard."

She keeps glancing up at the sky. The helicopter is very loud now, but she still can't see it. A few minutes ago, it sounded like it passed right overhead, and now it's circling back.

They're probably struggling to find the cabin because of the fog.

Had the air been clear, the helicopter would've surely landed twenty minutes ago, and they would both be in custody now. Veronica spent those ten minutes putting on her outer clothes—the pants in particular were tricky, and Molly had to help her because she couldn't bend her leg. Whenever she used the affected muscles even slightly, an avalanche of pain would roll through the entire leg, causing her to sweat and tremble and almost pass out. Fortunately, she found some morphine pills in the emergency suitcase and swallowed two with a glass of water; she can already feel them working. They're making her slightly woozy, but the pain is much less intense, and that's a big relief.

Another thing about the weather that's working to their advantage is that the temperature has risen to just above the freezing point. This means they won't freeze to death if the scooter runs out of gas. And she can already feel the snow scooter settling in better, so it'll probably be easier to drive.

"Come on," Veronica tells the girl. "Now you." Molly climbs onto the seat, putting her arms around Veronica's waist. The shotgun is between them; the feeling of it pressing against Veronica's back is reassuring. She brought the shells too, along with a battle of water and some beef jerky. All of it is crammed into her pockets, making the jacket heavy.

Just as she turns the gas handle, a light sweeps over them, and Molly gasps.

Veronica glances up and sees a silhouette of a helicopter hovering above the cabin. The searchlight goes back and forth, apparently trying to find a spot to land.

Veronica guns it, and the scooter takes off. She steers it out the driveway but doesn't follow the road—she doesn't need to. Instead, she heads straight in the direction of the harbor. She isn't entirely sure exactly how many miles they'll have to cover, but she hopes there might just be enough in the tank.

Soon, the sound of the helicopter fades to a background hum, and then it stops altogether.

Her phone is long dead, so Veronica has nothing to go on except her inner compass.

The fog has lifted a little, which allows her to up the speed.

It must be around noon, judging by how high the sun sits in the sky—which isn't very high at all, given that it's January.

They've passed two houses, but Veronica didn't stop to ask for help. She considers getting into contact with anybody a bad idea. For one thing, they're carrying the infection—Molly must be contagious by now. And for another, they're wanted by the police.

She asks Molly a question now and then—mostly to make sure the girl is still awake. She's shivering like a leaf. Veronica already stopped to give her an Aspirin and something to drink.

"They're not following us," Veronica tells Molly over her shoulder. "You can relax, sweetie."

Molly is shivering, but Veronica realizes it's not fear. The girl is pale, her eyes glassy.

She's spiking a fever. Already? Jeez ...

Veronica feels a gnawing dread settle in the pit of her stomach. The fungus, or whatever it is, is clearly working faster with every host it infects. Her own symptoms only came on in the evening after she'd touched the bird in the morning. That was, what, twelve hours? Leo, on the other hand, he started scratching already in the afternoon. And both Flemming and Alice had turned in a matter of—

"Look out!"

Molly's scream in her ear makes Veronica jolt, and they almost take a nosedive.

"What the heck, Molly? What are you—"

But then she sees it.

They've been passing a few trees, and sight visibility is so bad, Veronica isn't driving very fast. What she took to be just another tree is actually a person standing there in the snow. As they come closer, the figure becomes more visible through the fog, and Veronica recognizes Alice. Her figure is already transformed, most of her beautiful hair is gone, her arms too long, her frame too tall, but her nightclothes are what give her away.

Veronica steers clear, making a wide circle around Alice.

Molly whimpers.

Alice doesn't move, other than turning her head in order to follow them with her eyes. Veronica can tell she's smiling. She expects her to lunge at them any second.

But she doesn't.

And then she's gone.

"That ... that was my mom," Molly sobs.

"I know," Veronica tells her, swallowing hard. "I'm so sorry, Molly."

The girl begins crying. Veronica drives on, checking the mirror every three seconds.

Alice doesn't take up pursuit. Clearly, she let them go voluntarily. Did she know Molly was already infected? Most likely. But why didn't she attack Veronica? Try and eat her like Flemming had?

Veronica doesn't know.

But she really doesn't care for the smile she'd seen on Alice's face.

26

TIM

GETTING INTO THE CITY is a lot easier than he feared.

The soldiers seem to only be stationed by the roads, and since Tim is no longer driving, he simply runs out into the fields and crosses the city limit from there.

Once inside, he can move pretty much freely. As big and conspicuous as Tim is, none of the few people he meets seem to notice him. He expected a lot of police cars, helicopters overhead, soldiers in riot gear. But he sees none of that, and it soon becomes clear to him that the city is being abandoned. Not by civilians; those are told via radio, internet and loudspeakers to stay indoors and barricade themselves. But the authorities, police and military, are leaving.

They've given up. After Alan blew up, they decided to call it quits.

Tim gets it. From what Lundbeck told him, it sounded bad. Perhaps the authorities are even right to leave the city and simply try to contain the spread from the outside. Although he holds no illusions it will work. But at least they'll spare the lives of a lot of policemen and soldiers who would otherwise fight a losing battle against the ever-growing number of transforming people. Even with their protective gear and weapons, Tim is pretty sure they would serve as little more than food for the aliens.

The atmosphere in the city is extremely tense. Not only due to the empty streets and signs of fighting that's been going on—Tim can also feel the fear. He catches glimpses of faces staring out from windows, hears the occasional scream, and to make it even more eerie, he soon starts to pick up thoughts from the victims of the infection.

And there are a lot. Dozens. Hundreds, even. They're coming to him from different stages of the transformation and with different emotions. A few are reveling in their new powers. Some are confused. Most are scared.

Tim soon feels overwhelmed, and he makes a firm effort to shut out the signals, or he suspects his head will explode.

I need to find Buddy and get the hell out of here. Whole city's about to turn into a huge lion cage.

As he jogs through the streets, he feels bad for the people hunkering down in their homes. Regular residences won't provide much protection against the horde of flesh-hungry aliens that are about to ravage through the city. He gets why the authorities feel the need to lie to them, but it also makes him angry. The shot-callers in Copenhagen probably know the cause is lost and are planning a nationwide lockdown and military takeover. Sealing off Hornstedt, effectively sacrificing twenty thousand people, will buy them a few more days to prepare the rest of the country while the aliens feast on the locals.

Tim only has a handful of friends who live in Hornstedt, so it's not really anything personal. It's his moral compass that's objecting. Twenty thousand people is a lot of sacrificial lambs.

People should be allowed to leave. Or at least get the choice.

But he can't see a way to make that happen. Unless—

His thoughts are abruptly cut off as a woman comes bolting out from behind a parked van. She's wearing regular clothes, no jacket or shoes, and she's looking back with horror on her face. "No! No, stay away from me!"

Through the van's windows, Tim catches a glimpse of an older, half-transformed guy wearing nothing but his boxers chasing her, and he instinctively jumps forward and clotheslines the guy as he comes into view. Tim's arm catches him below the chin, and he almost spins all the way around before crashing to the pavement. Not giving him a chance to get up, Tim bends over and punches him twice in the back on the head, then stomps his heel down on the base of the guy's skull, hearing the spinal cord crunch. The guy gives one last groan, twitches, then lies still.

Tim looks in the direction of the woman. She's stopped on the other side of the street. She looks like she wants to keep running.

"It's okay," Tim tells her. "He's done."

The woman's hand goes to her mouth. "He ... he was my father-in-law."

"I'm sorry," Tim says. "Go back inside. Don't trust anyone who's infected. They'll become like him sooner or later." He gestures at the dead guy.

The woman just stares at him wide-eyed. Then, waking her from her stupor, comes a kid's voice: "Mom? Mooom?"

"I'm here, honey!" she calls, running back the way she came. "I'm okay! Go back into the house!"

Tim sees her lift up the girl waiting for her in the doorway. She can't be older than four. Then the woman slams the door.

Tim breathes hard through his nose.

He makes up his mind. He's not leaving this place until he's done something to help the people still alive here.

27

VERONICA

THE PAIN IN HER leg is still only a dull ache, and as long as she doesn't move it, it's tolerable. She's deep in gloomy thoughts about what the hell she's going to do once—if ever—they reach the harbor, when suddenly, a wall of snow appears up ahead. It's not a natural dune—it's clearly made by a plow. It's too tall for her to look over, and it seems to go around in a circle.

Veronica stops and takes off her beanie in order to hear better. Over the hum of the engine, she can make out the sound of other vehicles. She kills the scooter.

"Why are we stopping?" Molly croaks.

"Shhh," Veronica shushes. "I need you to climb up and tell me what's on the other side of the snow. Can you do that for me?"

Molly nods and slips off the scooter. She hugs herself as though freezing, but she nonetheless goes to the wall of snow and scales it. Peeking over the top, she comes back down a few moments later.

"I think it's the harbor," she says, wiping away a stray tear. "There's a lot of cars. I think they're waiting to drive aboard the ferry. It was difficult to see because of the fog."

Veronica feels a surge of relief. Sniffing, she can smell salt in the air, which must mean they're by the water. "Great," she says. "That's great news. We made it. So far so good."

Molly just stands there, trembling. "So, do we just drive on it?"

Veronica considers it briefly. They could probably get Molly on to the ferry without raising any eyebrows—except for thin rim below her eyes which looks more like makeup, nothing's visibly growing on her. It'll be a lot harder to get Veronica onboard without anybody noticing how badly wounded she is. And as soon as the staff finds out, they'll surely call a doctor and maybe also the police.

"Did you see any police officers?" Veronica asks.

Molly nods. "There were two, no, three police cars over there."

Veronica bites down hard. "Damnit. They're probably evacuating the island."

"Isn't that a good thing?" Molly asks. "I really want to go, Veronica. So I can lie down and stop freezing."

"I know, sweetie. But I bet they're checking everyone going onboard, and if they find out you have a fever …" She can tell from Molly's expression she doesn't need to explain further.

"So, what do we do?" the girl asks.

Veronica bites her frozen lip. "You said there was a line of cars?"

"Uh-huh."

"Were they coming from this side?" She points to the left—the direction facing away from the water.

"Uh-huh."

"Come on, then. Get back on."

"Where are we going?" Molly asks, climbing on behind Veronica.

Veronica turns the scooter's engine back on. "We're hitching a ride."

28

VERONICA

SNAKING AROUND THE MOUND of snow, they soon reach the road and the entrance point to the harbor.

Molly was right. The cars really are lined up, waiting for their turn to drive onboard the ferry.

Veronica stops behind a couple of fir trees and shuts the engine off. She can see a police car parked by the side of the road. The officer, clad in a heavy coat, boots, trapper hat, and a face mask, is going from vehicle to vehicle with what looks to be a laser gun. He points it at the driver and any passengers, then moves on.

"They're checking people's temperatures," Veronica mutters. "Clever."

She's both relieved to see the authorities taking things seriously, but also worried about the fact that she'll have to break the law and risk getting caught.

Apparently, Molly has the same concern, because she says in a low voice: "Maybe ... maybe we should just go and talk with the police?"

"No," Veronica says firmly—it's almost a snarl, and she surprises herself by how determined she sounds. "No," she tells the girl a little softer. "They can't help you, Molly. The doctor who came to the cabin ... he said it himself; they don't know what this is."

"So … what are we gonna do?" Molly asks, sounding even more uneasy. "Am I going to …?"

Veronica turns around to look at her. "Hey. Don't think like that. I'm gonna make it all right, okay? I'm gonna figure something out. I have too, because I'm the one who—" Her voice breaks, and she's suddenly on the verge of tears. Biting down hard, she goes on, "We're getting you to the mainland, and then we'll go to the hospital. I have a friend there; she works as a nurse. She'll help us." Veronica didn't know this was the plan before she said it out loud, but hearing it, she feels a little better about the whole thing. It actually makes sense. Her friend, Luna, works at one of the best cancer centers in the country, and she won't turn down Veronica—she owes her a big favor after what Veronica did for her when she—

The sound of a whistle makes Veronica spin back around and duck. Her hand goes for the ignition, and she almost turns the scooter back on. She's expecting the cop to come running for them, but he's still by the row of cars. He's opened the driver's door of a black station wagon and is waving at someone farther up ahead.

"Please step out of the car, lady," Veronica hears him tell the driver. "I'm not saying it nicely again."

A woman old enough to be Veronica's mom, wearing an expensive fur coat and silky gloves, steps out reluctantly. She's shaking her head, causing her grey, neatly combed hair to sway. Inside the car, on the passenger seat, Veronica sees a cage with a Maltese dog in it. It's barking shrilly at the officer.

"I'm—I'm telling you, I'm not sick," the woman says, her voice breaking. "This is just silly … Please, I assure you, there's no need for this."

The officer doesn't answer. He steps back and keeps his arm outstretched, clearly telling the woman not to approach him. From the side comes two men dressed in full hazmat suits. They're not carrying any medical equipment; instead, they bring handcuffs.

"Fever?" one of them asks through the mask.

"No, but the dog," the first officer says, pointing inside the car. "Its fur is riddled with that black stuff."

"It's just lint from my carpet," the woman says, laughing nervously. "He rolled around on it this morning just as we were leaving. I'm telling you—"

"Please turn around and put your hands together on your back," one of the hazmat suits tells the woman.

She keeps babbling about how her dog isn't sick at all, until the men lose patience and grab her. They put the cuffs on her and drag her off. Surprisingly, they don't move towards the ferry, but away from it. There's an ambulance parked behind the row of cars. They open the back doors, and Veronica sees a man in there, sitting with his hands behind his back. They put the woman in the back of the ambulance too, then close the doors again. One of the suits exchange a brief word with the driver, and then the ambulance heads off.

"See?" Veronica says grimly over her shoulder. "They're not curing the sick. They're just containing them. And they don't get to leave the island."

Molly swallows and nods.

Veronica sees the suits and the officer returning to the woman's car. The dog is still barking.

"What about that thing?" the officer asks.

One of the suits shrugs. "Put it down."

"No," Veronica whispers. "Just leave it alone. It'll be fine in a couple of hours."

"Really?" the officer asks, taking out his gun. "You want me to just—"

"Of course not, Bjarne," the suit snaps, grabbing the cop's wrist. He glances around, then says in a lower voice that Veronica barely makes out over the idling engines. "Not in front of everybody."

The cop nods, puts the gun back in the holster. Then he comes around the car, opens the passenger door and takes out the cage. The dog barks louder and tries to bite him through the grid.

"Whoa," the cop says. "Easy, boy. We're just going for a stroll. Calm down."

He looks from side to side, trying to decide where to do it. Then he sees a patch of trees a little off to the side—the opposite side of where Veronica and Molly are—and he leaves the road. One of the suits gets in behind the wheel, and the other signals to the car behind it to back up so they can get the woman's car out of the way.

"What's he doing with the dog?" Molly asks.

"Never mind," Veronica tells her, even though she feels bad for the poor animal too. "He'll be gone for a minute or two. And the others are occupied too. This is our chance. Come on."

The get off the scooter, and Veronica leads the way through the snow, limping and wincing with every step. Luckily, the morphine is really doing the trick now—her leg hurts, but not nearly as bad. As soon as they leave the trees, they're visible to anyone inside the cars, but people are either busy staring at their phones or up ahead.

They reach the last car and run behind it. It's an SUV with an old guy behind the wheel.

Standing in an awkward bent-over position, Veronica hands the gun to Molly and whispers, "You stay here. I'll be right back." Then she straightens up and walks to the driver's side door as casually as she can, hoping the guy won't look in the mirror and notice her limp.

He doesn't notice, because he's talking to someone on the phone.

Veronica taps the window, and he jolts, almost dropping his cell. Veronica smiles at him. "I'm sorry," she says loudly, "but they told me you tell you ..."

The guy squints and rolls down the window half an inch. "Wha'?"

"They told me to tell you," Veronica says again, nodding towards the front of the car. "Your license plate. They can't read it. It's covered with snow."

"Arh, damn them," the guy growls. A nerve twitches at the corner of his mouth. "Yeah, hang on, son. They want me to clear the license plate. Gimme a sec."

As the guy puts down the phone, he begins fumbling with his seat belt and putting on his gloves, Veronica moves discreetly back to the rear of the car. And as he gets out, she opens the cargo area and ushers Molly inside. Bringing the gun, the girl climbs in, then helps Veronica. In order to do so, she needs to bend her leg slightly, and a fire bolt of pain almost makes her cry out. She manages to stifle the sound, and then they're in the car. She closes the door just as she sees another pair of headlights come out of the fog as the next car joins the cue.

Three seconds later, the old guy gets back in behind the wheel, causing the car to sway gently.

He grunts with annoyance. "You still there? ... Yeah, it didn't even have any snow on it ... Typical ... No, I think we'll be leaving within the hour, least that's what they told us last ... Yeah, I know ... Well, tell her not to worry, then ..."

Veronica looks around quietly. It's hot in the car, and the cargo area is pretty crammed. Luckily, the guy didn't bring a lot of stuff, or there wouldn't have been enough room for Veronica and Molly.

But there's a bigger problem: There's nothing hiding them. It's only now Veronica realizes this hole in her plan. Had they had a blanket or something, they could've hidden under that. But as soon as the cop looks in through the back window, he'll see them lying there.

"Yeah, I think they're waving me forward now," the old guy says. "Finally!"

The car starts moving. Veronica zips down her jacket a few inches—just enough to pull it up over her face. She looks at Molly and whispers: "You do the same. We need to hide our faces. Maybe they won't see us."

Molly's hand goes to her zipper, but then she appears to get a better idea. She looks up, reaches up her hand, takes hold of a handle that's sticking out from the back of the seat, and then she gently pulls out a cover. It goes all the way across, forming a perfect ceiling over their heads. Molly fastens it and looks at Veronica in the darkness with a shy smile.

"How'd you know about that?" Veronica whispers.

"We have a car just like this one," Molly says.

"Oh," Veronica smiles. "Great job, Molly."

The car stops again, and Veronica hears someone tap a window.

"Yeah, yeah," the old guy grunts.

She hears him roll down the window, and the cop says something about "body temperature." There's a pause, a beep, then the cop says, "You're cleared."

The old guy rolls the window back up, and the car moves forward again.

Veronica looks at Molly again. "They didn't even check."

Molly lets out a low, trembling sigh of relief. Veronica can smell citrous on her breath, and her short-lived relief is replaced by worry.

It's in her lungs. How long has she got?

29

TIM

HE REACHES ALAN'S HOUSE ten minutes later.

Tim's truck is still there, right where he parked it. He goes to check if Buddy is in the back. He's not.

Tim didn't bother locking the truck. In fact, he left the key in the hidden compartment below the wheel. The police no doubt searched through the truck, but when Tim opens the door and reaches for the key, he finds it. He then reaches under the seat and finds his Glock, too.

Huh. Maybe they didn't bother searching it after all.

Slipping the gun down the back of his pants, he goes to the front door. The lights are on in there, and Alan's Mercedes is parked in the carport. Tim knows how fond his friend was of that car; he got it just last year.

"Sorry again, pal," Tim mutters.

He tries the handle, but the door is locked. He knows Alan has an expensive security system, and if he tries to break open the door, it'll sound the alarm. Not that he's worried about the police showing up, but he doesn't want to draw too much attention. Glancing around, he makes sure the street is empty. Most of the windows of the other houses have lights in them, but no one's outside.

The air raid alarm sounds again, followed by the message Tim has heard four times now: "To everyone hearing this: This is an official statement. Seek refuge indoors. Lock doors and windows. Protect yourself. Help is on its way."

It repeats a few times, then falls quiet.

Tim leans closer to the door and says, "Buddy? You in there?"

No answer.

Tim goes around to the bathroom window, hoping to find it open like he left it. It's been locked. He can easily smash it, of course, but he still prefers not sounding the alarm unless he has to. So instead, he—

"Mister? Hey, Mister?"

Tim spins around to see a boy peering out from the corner of the house. He's ten or eleven, and he sounds anxious.

"You came for your dog?" the boy asks. "We've got him back here. Come on, come with me."

The boy waves at him twice, then disappears from sight.

Tim doesn't at first. He stays where he is, aware that every alarm bell is ringing in his head.

The boy wasn't transformed. For one thing, he was able to talk just fine, and Tim could also make out his features despite the darkness, and there were no signs of the infection. He also didn't pick up on any lemony smells from the boy.

Still ... something's wrong. He's sure of it.

I've got no choice, Tim thinks, biting down hard. He doesn't immediately follow the boy, but runs back to the carport. On the wall hangs a tire iron. Tim grabs it and then runs to the corner where he saw the boy.

Carefully stepping into Alan's backyard, Tim keeps his senses at high alert. The lawn is grey below the moonlight. He immediately spots the boy. He's by the pavilion at the far end. It's beautifully built in wood and has big windows on both sides. At the front is the door, and it's closed. Behind it, Tim can hear Buddy breathing.

Spotting him, the boy gestures at the door. "He's right in here, Mister. We've kept him safe for you."

"Who's 'we'?" Tim asks, focusing most of his attention on his peripheral vision and hearing. He's picking up no movements, no sounds. He can smell aliens, though, but that could be coming from anywhere; a mild breeze is stirring, and there's got to be at least a few fully transformed people in the city by now.

"Me and ... my dad," the boy says, obviously lying. He gestures at the door again. "You can go get him now. He's right in there."

Tim watches the boy for a moment. He's wearing shoes and a thick jacket, but he's still shivering. He looks more than anxious—he's terrified. Tim is still certain the boy isn't infected, but he's clearly being used as a puppet for someone who is.

"Is there anybody else in the pavilion besides my dog?" Tim asks.

"No," the boy says right away. "Just your dog. Please, go in there and get him."

"Is he okay?" Tim asks calmly. "No one hurt him?"

"No," the boy says, shaking his head. "No, he's fine."

As though confirming this, Tim hears Buddy getting to his feet. He can hear him hold his breath, as though listening.

"It's me, Buddy," Tim says a little louder. "You all right?"

Buddy gives a quick series of barks. He sounds fine. Eager to see Tim. But also tense. As though he's seen something alarming.

Scanning the frozen lawn, Tim sees several footprints in front of the pavilion. He can't tell if they're all human. But he can also make out tiny tufts of Buddy's fur. Meaning the dog clearly didn't go in the pavilion voluntarily.

Tim comes closer, stopping ten steps from the pavilion. "I want you to open the door," he tells the boy.

The boy jolts. "Me? But I ... okay." He grabs the handle and opens the door.

Buddy is in there, between the tipped over garden chairs, tied with a rope to the center support post. Judging by the state of the rope, Buddy hasn't been in there for long, or he would have chewed through it by now. He begins whining at the sight of Tim.

"Hey, Buddy," Tim says. "You okay?"

Buddy shakes his fur and whines some more.

"You've seen somethin'?" Tim asks him.

Buddy gives a single, sharp bark.

"Please, mister," the boy pleads. "Can you just go and get him? I want to get home."

"Sure," Tim says, stepping closer. He's no longer in any doubt that this is a trap. But he can tell no one else is inside the pavilion, and there are no explosives or anything else. So, whatever the danger is, it'll come from outside the pavilion. Probably the moment he steps inside. "I just need to ask him one more thing," Tim goes on, looking at Buddy as his hand goes to the gun. "Where are they, Buddy? Where'd you see 'em?"

Buddy whips around and goes as far as the rope allows him, then he gets on his hindlegs and flails both front paws towards the back of the pavilion.

"Oh, they're hiding behind the back?" Tim says loudly, taking a step back. "That's not very cunning."

Even as he speaks, he can hear someone behind the pavilion start to move. The frozen grass crunches below their feet as they come around each side of the building, upping their speed.

"Get out of the way," Tim hisses at the boy as he whips out the Glock and fires at the alien appearing on his left first. It's a male, little more than half-transformed, very young; not much more than a big teenager. Tim catches him in the neck with two bullets, and he screeches and drops.

Jumping farther back, Tim pans the gun right and fires just as the other alien lunges for him—this one is a grown man, farther transformed and bigger. Tim fires at him point-blank in the chest four times, and it's enough to throw him off course. Still, Tim has to move sideways to avoid getting clawed by the guy on his way down. He shoots him twice more in the back of the head, then spins around and fires again at the teenager who's crawling towards Tim, hissing and gurgling. A bullet goes right through the crown of his head, sending him to the ground.

Tim pans all the way around, making sure no one else is approaching from any direction. The garden is empty. He can't hear anyone coming, either.

Buddy is barking and the boy is crying. He goes to the teenager, bows his head and covers his face in his hands.

Tim puts away the gun and goes and puts a hand on the boy's shoulder. He jumps and pulls away.

"It's okay," Tim tells him.

"No," the boy says, sniffing. "It's not okay. That's Michael, my brother. And my dad ... you killed them."

"I'm really sorry," Tim says. "They were already dead, son."

The boy bursts into tears and hides his face again. "They ... they made me do it ..." He says between sobs.

"I know, don't worry about it. Where do you live?"

The boy gestures north. "A few houses down the road."

"Is anyone in your family still alive?"

"My mom. And my grandpa."

"Are they at the house?"

"Uh-huh."

"Are they infected?"

The boy stops crying briefly to look at Tim. "No. Dad didn't touch them. He only touched Michael."

"That's good. Go back home, then."

The boy doesn't need to be told a second time; he runs out of the garden.

Tim goes and unties Buddy. The dog almost knocks him over. "Easy, pal. I'm glad to see you too."

They go out to the truck, and Buddy immediately jumps in when Tim opens the door. He gets in behind the wheel himself, and just as he does, he picks up another radio signal. It's a random conversation between two policemen. Tim doesn't bother to listen. But it gives him an idea.

I can pick up. But can I send out, too?

Turning on the truck, he places his palm on the radio. He feels a bit silly doing so, and he's aware that Buddy is eyeing him from the back. "I know, I know," Tim mutters. "Just ... let me give it a shot."

Staring out the windscreen, Tim concentrates. He opens his mind to the many signals darting back and forth. And then he feels it. The connection. Opening his mouth, he's not exactly sure what he should say, so he decides to go with the truth. "People of Hornstedt ..."

A second later, the words echo out over the air raid speakers.

Holy shit, Tim thinks. *It's really working.*

He clears his throat. "People of Hornstedt. You shouldn't believe what the authorities are telling you. The city is riddled with infected folks. They will eat every last one of you. It's up to you whether you want to hunker down and try and defend yourself, or whether you want to flee. But don't count on the police or the military; they're already leaving." He hesitates, listening to the message as it repeats all over town. Then he adds: "Help each other. Save yourselves. No one else can."

Then he takes his hand off the radio and feels a brief, static shock as the connection is broken.

He glances at Buddy. "I know that wasn't a lot, but at least it was something." He puts it in drive. "Come on, now. Let's go home."

30

VERONICA

"Veronica?"

She's called awake by Molly's voice close to her ear. Grunting, Veronica tries to sit up but is immediately reminded of her leg wound by a fierce pain. She barely manages to hold back a scream.

"We're still in the back of the car," Molly whispers, placing her hands on Veronica's shoulders. "You can't get up right now."

Veronica rubs her eyes and tries to see the girl in the dimness. Only a faint light comes down from the crack in the cover. Veronica is sitting in an awkward mermaid posture which she apparently was also sleeping in. Her good leg is prickling from having the blood flow restricted, and her lower back aches almost more than the bite wound.

"Still on the ferry?" Veronica mutters.

Molly places a finger over her lips and gestures towards the front of the car. "He's still here."

"Oh." Listening, Veronica can hear the radio going. And what she took to be rumbling from the ferry is really the car's idling engine. She assumed the man had left the car while on the ferry, but evidently, he didn't.

"I don't think they're allowed to leave the cars," Molly whispers, answering Veronica's unspoken question. "They said something over the speakers. I think we're about to go ashore. That's why he turned the car back on."

Veronica nods and tries to make out Molly's face. "How're you doing?"

The girl shrugs. "I'm fine."

And she does look fine. *Suspiciously* fine. Veronica reaches out a hand and strokes Molly's cheek. She tugs her earlobe, runs her thumb across her lips, and gently touches her below both eyes. Molly's skin is smooth and clean. "The black stuff?" Veronica whispers.

Molly shrugs again. "I don't know. It just ... went away."

"It did?" Veronica can't help but raise her voice a little, and Molly shushes her again. By now, however, several other engines are humming all around them, and Veronica doubts the old guy could hear them even if they spoke at normal volume.

"Yeah. I drifted off for a little while. I don't know how long, but when I woke back up, I felt much better. And I can't find it anywhere on my body."

"That's ... incredible," Veronica says, surveying Molly closely. She really wishes she could see her face better. Read her expression. Her voice sounds unchanged.

Why did the stuff go away so quickly? It could be taken as good news, but instead it creates a nagging feeling in the pit of Veronica's stomach.

Molly pretty much skipped the fever state. No going comatose like the others. Which means that either she kicked it, or ...

It's moving a lot faster in her.

"Listen," Veronica whispers, leaning closer, trying discreetly to get a better look of Molly's eyes. "You say you're feeling better, and that's good. But ... do you feel like yourself?"

Molly blinks once. "What do you mean?"

"Well ... has anything changed inside of you? Your thoughts, your feelings. Do you still feel like Molly?"

The girl blinks again. "Who else would I feel like?"

Veronica doesn't get a chance to answer, because the guy behind the wheel suddenly grunts. "That's about time." Then the car starts moving. They drive slowly forward. There's a bump. They drive down at a fairly steep angle. Veronica recalls the boarding ramp, and a few seconds later, they're driving on asphalt. She can tell the light coming in is a bit brighter now.

"Okay," Veronica whispers, feeling a brief sense of relief. "We made it. We're on the mainland."

"That's great," Molly whispers—her tone neutral.

"So now we're in Frederikshavn," Veronica goes on, thinking out loud. "The clinic where Luna works is at the north end of town. It's only twenty minutes away."

"But ... we don't know where he's going," Molly whispers, nodding towards the driver.

The guy's phone rings. They hear him mutter to himself, then the phone stops ringing, and he says loudly: "Yeah?"

The person on the other end is a man, and he's on speaker. *"Dad, it's me. How long till you get here?"*

"Hold your horses. I just got off the damn boat. It'll be another hour. I'm headed for you guys now."

"Great. Because the kids are crawling up the walls. And Mom keeps saying we won't make it. I think she's got a point, you know; I think it's just a matter of time before they close the borders. So maybe you—"

"Look, damnit, I'm going as fast as I can," the man snaps. "I was lucky they even let us off the freaking island."

"But maybe we should call a cab and get moving? You could meet up with us at—"

"Stop talking nonsense! Who's gonna pay for a three-hundred-mile cab ride? You? Besides, getting into a cab will let all the neighbors know something is wrong. I'm sure people are already on edge; if we get them all riled up, the authorities will definitely close the borders, and then we ain't going nowheres."

"But—"

"I told you, I'm coming for y'all. Just make sure you've got everything. Bring as much food as you can, the kind that'll last. I'm only an hour away. Tell your mom to simmer the hell down."

A brief pause. *"Okay, Dad."*

"See you soon."

The call is ended.

Veronica and Molly look at each other.

"Okay," Veronica whispers, taking the gun. "Time for the next part of the plan."

Molly's eyes flash in the darkness. "Are you gonna shoot him?"

"No. Of course not. But we need to get you to the clinic, and I doubt he'll take us there voluntarily." Veronica aims the barrel of the gun at the hatch, then makes sure the safety is off. "Move over," she whispers. "As far away from me as you can."

Molly scooches to the side, allowing Veronica to have a clean angle in which to fire the gun without risking hitting the girl. She doesn't want to fire it, but she might need to. The old guy is obviously a tough nut, and Veronica is in no position to handle him in a physical scuffle. The gun is her only ace, and she needs to at the very least make the guy think that she's willing to fire it.

Veronica purses her lips and whistles softly.

No reaction from the driver.

She whistles a little louder. He grunts and turns down the radio.

Veronica waits with bated breath.

But the guy keeps driving, so she gives a third whistle.

"What the heck?" the guy mutters. The car starts to slow down, and Veronica sends Molly a significant look, mouthing, "Be ready—don't move."

The guy stops the car, pulls the handbrake, and then apparently sits and listens for a few seconds. Veronica hears another car approaching and passing them by. Judging by the speed of it, they're already on the highway. Which is good. Means there are probably fewer houses or pedestrians around. Fewer witnesses.

Apparently, the guy decides the sound came from the engine or something and that's it's gone now, because he mumbles something, then puts the car back into drive.

As they begin rolling, Veronica whistles again, louder this time.

"What the heck?" the guy exclaims, stomping the brake. "Someone back there?"

He yanks the handbrake once more, then unbuckles. He opens the door and gets out, causing the car to sway gently. Veronica hears his footsteps come around to the back. There's a click, and the hatch opens.

The daylight is much brighter than she anticipated, and Veronica has no choice but to squint her eyes almost shut. She can just make out the guy's frame, and she jabs the barrel into his belly. "Don't move. Don't say a word. Stay absolutely still, or I'll blow out your gut. Don't think I won't."

Her voice breaks because of how tense she is, but it only adds a sense of desperation to the words, and the guy freezes. She can't see his face because of the cover, and his hands are out of sight, too—one of them still holding the hatch, the other hanging by his side.

"Remove the cover," Veronica demands. "Slowly. No tricks. I've got my finger on the trigger."

"Listen here, lady," the guy begins, that annoying nerve twitching at the corner of his mouth again. "I don't know what you want, but I—"

"I want you to remove the fucking cover like I told you, and keep your mouth shut."

The guy grunts, but he does as he's told. Using the hand that held the hatch, he clicks the cover free and allows it to roll back into place. He leans a little forward, the gun pressing into his jacket. "I can't ... I can't reach any farther," he says.

"Just let it go," Veronica says, blinking away tears. Her eyes are slowly adjusting to the light and she's better able to focus. They really are on a highway, and seeing the naked trees on one side of the road, Veronica can immediately tell the mainland didn't get nearly as much snow as the Islé of Heir did.

The old guy releases the cover, and it rolls all the way back, snapping into place.

Veronica strains her eyes to see his face. He looks from her to Molly, only now realizing the girl is there, too. "What the hell are you two doing in my trunk?"

Another car comes up from behind, but it doesn't even slow down. The old guy just looks like he's gotten out to fetch something from the back.

"We need to get somewhere," Veronica says. "We're going there now. You can either drive us there, or you can stay right here at the side of the road. Which option do you prefer?"

The guy squints—not because of the daylight, but because he gets angry. "You've got a lot of nerve, lady."

"That's not what I asked," Veronica says, sitting up a bit farther. She wants to get into a better position in case the guy tries to make a move. Her leg gives off a jolt of pain, and she winces.

"You're hurt," the old guy notices. "That's a bad wound you've got there."

"Take a step back," Veronica snarls through gritted teeth.

"Veronica," Molly whispers.

"Be quiet," Veronica tells her without taking her eyes off the guy, regretting that the girl just revealed her name. "I'll do the talking. You, step back. Now!"

The guy doesn't step back. Instead, he gestures at Veronica's leg. "If you don't get that looked at soon, it'll fester. I can call you an ambulance if you want?"

"Veronica, I think he's—"

"Shut up!" Veronica hisses. "Both of you." She blinks hard and stares at the guy. "If you don't get back now, I swear to God, I'm pulling the trigger."

The guy sighs as though about to comply.

Then two things happen in close succession.

First, Molly screams out: "He's got a weapon!" And then the guy raises the hand that's been out of sight until now. It looks like a sawed-off wooden bat. He pushes aside the gun with the free hand, then swings the piece of wood at Veronica.

She expects him to aim for her head, and so she instinctively covers her face. But the club doesn't go near her head. Instead, the guy slams it down on her bad leg, connecting right above the knee, three inches from her wound.

Veronica screams out as intense pain explodes and immediately sets her entire leg on fire. She pulls the trigger, not sure where the gun is aimed, and the shot wipes out her hearing. She feels shattered glass rain down over her, and she sees the guy stagger backwards, his hands going to his face. He's apparently unhurt, only surprised, because he comes forward almost right away. Veronica—her entire body trembling with pain, her brain on the verge of passing out—manages to lower the gun and aim it at his chest. But just as she fires the second round, the guy reaches her and slaps the barrel aside once more.

He leans in, raises the club, and hisses something Veronica can't make out. Then, just as he's about to club her again, this time clearly aiming for her head, something comes flying into view from the side. Molly throws herself into the arms of the guy, causing him to stumble backwards. He fights to get her off as she apparently claws away at his face.

Veronica—only halfway conscious—fumbles out the box of shells and loads two more into the gun. Then she scooches to the edge of the cargo area, letting both legs swing to the ground, ignoring another wave of pain. Staying seated, she places the gun against her shoulder and calls out, "Get off him, Molly!"

Her shout is redundant, because the guy wrestles Molly off just then, and she falls to the frozen ground with a thud. Snarling and sprawling, she gets up immediately and is about to attack the guy again, when Veronica shouts, "*Molly! Stop!*"

The girl whips around to glare at her, and Veronica gasps. Molly is a terrifying sight.

Around her mouth is fresh blood. For an awful second, it looks to Veronica as though the girl got a nasty punch to the mouth. But then she sees her eyes, and she realizes it's not Molly's blood at all.

Dear God ...

Molly's eyes have faded—one more so than the other.

Veronica looks back at the old guy, who's still just standing there. He sways as though his legs threaten to buckle. His hand goes to his face, touches his cheek carefully. It's torn open and bleeding badly. There are deep cuts in his eyebrow, forehead and along his jawline, too. And on the side of his neck is a missing piece of skin where Molly took a bite. Blood is gushing out, splattering to the ground.

"You little ... crazy ... bitch," the guy mumbles, looking at his bloody hand. Then his eyes close and he collapses.

31

VERONICA

For several long seconds, none of them move.

The old guy just lies there, bleeding out on the ground.

Veronica sits on the edge of the car, hearing nothing but her own throbbing pulse.

Molly is standing a few feet away, wiping the blood off her face with her hand. She looks at the blood, her expression going back and forth between lust and disgust. It looks like she's trying to decide whether she wants to lick the blood from her hand or not. Veronica wants to say something, wants to scream at Molly not to do it, but she can't get a word out. The pain is still keeping her on the verge of passing out.

Apparently, though, whatever humanity still resides in the girl wins in the end, because she lowers her hand and sends Veronica a guilty look. "I didn't mean to kill him."

Veronica reads the words from her lips. She just shakes her head and looks down the road. A pair of headlights is approaching in the distance. Had a car passed by in the last thirty seconds or so, they would no doubt have seen what was going on at the roadside. But, luckily, traffic is very sparse this early evening.

"Someone's coming," Veronica hears herself say. "We better get him out of sight."

She can't do it. She can barely stand up, let alone drag a body.

To her surprise, Molly jumps on the task. The girl grabs the guy around the wrists and, leaning back, she grunts as she pulls him around to the side of the car. Even though the ground is frozen, she shouldn't be able to move a fully grown man. But she does.

And as she returns, the car reaches them and slows down.

A young, Black guy rolls down the window. "Hey, you guys need help?"

"We're fine," Veronica hears herself say, blinking. "Thank you."

"Because, you know, I've got jumper cables ..." He gestures with his thumb towards his trunk.

"Our car is fine," Veronica says, crossing her arms as she tries to smile. "We're just ... resting."

"Oh. Right." The guy gives her a once-over, then looks at Molly. It seems like he's trying to discern whether anything fishy is going on. "You guys know there's just been a curfew, right? You can't leave town."

"Oh," Veronica says, realizing why there are so few cars on the road. "No, we know," she says. "We're headed back."

The guy moves his jaw. "You sure you're all right?"

"Yep, we're fine," Molly tells him, sending him a genuine smile. Veronica's hearing is almost back to normal by now, and she can tell Molly's voice is different. Higher. More screechy. To the guy, it probably just sounds like Molly hit puberty or has a sore throat.

"Okay, then," he says, nodding. "You take care, then."

He rolls his window back up and drives on.

Veronica looks down to see a big, glistening pool of blood. It's visible from where she stands, but the Black guy didn't notice it because the asphalt is so dark. Also, the daylight is already fading.

She looks at Molly. "You okay?"

The girl sniffs, nods, looks away, then looks back at Veronica.

"What is it, Molly?" Veronica is afraid of the answer.

Molly shrugs. "I'm not ... I'm not sure this is a good idea."

"What isn't a good idea?"

Molly sniffs again, turns her upper body and looks towards the trees, like she's longing to go. It's freezing cold, and Veronica shivers despite the parka. Molly, on the other hand, looks very comfortable in the cold air.

"Molly?"

"Hmm?" Molly looks back at Veronica as though she forgot she was even there. For a second, her eyes look weird. As though she's not looking at Veronica at all, but something else entirely. Something ... appetizing. Then it's gone.

"What isn't a good idea?" Veronica asks.

"Us," Molly says bluntly. "Being together. I feel ... I feel strange, Veronica."

Veronica bites her lip. "Listen, sweetie. We're getting you to the doctor, and we'll fix you. I swear."

Molly hesitates, then gives a little nod.

"Get in the car," Veronica says, getting up with a wince. "It's got automatic gears. I should be able to drive it."

32

HELENA

IT'S STILL DARK WHEN she reaches the cabin.

Parking the truck on the lot in front of the house, she kills the engine and switches off the light. She sits for a moment, takes in the sight of her childhood home. It looks almost exactly the same, only more worn. The windows could use a good cleaning, and the roof is heavy with moss. The front door is closed and there are no lights on in there. She takes that as a good sign.

Getting out of the car, she shudders as an icy gust of wind greets her. She glances across the meadow. The trees are black skeletons against the gray sky.

It's over there somewhere. The rock, or whatever it is.

As a kid, Helena would often play in the forest. It's some of her fondest memories. Whether it's just because she knows about the strange object, or if she can really sense it out there, she can't tell. Either way, looking in the direction of the forest makes her anxious.

She brings the key to the front door. Just as she sticks it in the lock, another breeze blows by, and something white comes tumbling across her shoes. Looking down, she sees what looks like a down feather. It's followed by another one, and another. Helena crouches down and picks up one of them. It's smeared in what can only be blood.

Looking in the direction where the feathers came from, Helena gasps.

She has seen bird carcasses before, whenever a fox or a hawk had surprised and killed a pigeon, and she knows it usually includes a lot of loose feathers scattered around.

But what she sees is more like if someone cut open a big pillow and emptied it all over the grass.

Hundreds of feathers are littering the lawn, some of them moving with the breeze. The trail is coming from the henhouse. The door is ajar, as though her dad forgot to close it.

Helena's heart is beating faster now.

It's probably just a fox. They're clever. It could've figured out how to jump up and pull the handle.

Another gust of wind carries with it the unmistakable smell of chicken blood—Helena recognizes it from when her dad would slaughter a rooster for dinner.

She stands there, in front of the door to the cabin, uncertain about what to do. The wind dies down for a brief moment, and the night falls completely quiet. In the silence, she seems to hear a low rattle coming from the henhouse.

It could be the door moving gently on the hinges. Or it could be something breathing in there. A chicken that hasn't been killed properly? Or the predator that did the killing? Is it still in there?

Helena feels a strong urge to pee. Something about the situation is scaring her. She keeps telling herself it's just a fox or a badger, but she can't quite convince herself.

She wants to call up her dad, but he specifically asked her not to, unless absolutely necessary, because turning on her phone would mean the authorities could track her to the cabin, and they might still be looking for him—although Helena assumes they have more important things to focus on now. Still, she doesn't want to bother him if it turns out it's just a runaway dog who came by and feasted on the birds.

What would Dad say if he was here?

The answer is obvious. He'd tell her to go hide in the basement while he himself went to the coop to check it out.

But the thought of her cowering underground without at least knowing for certain what happened to the chickens—that's enough to make her claustrophobic. She needs to know.

She leaves the key in the door, and, holding her breath, she walks along the trail of feathers, approaching the henhouse. The smell of blood and guts becomes stronger. She strains her eyes to see through the crack in the door, but it's very dark in there. Leaning forward, she squints to make out the shadows inside.

There's hardly anything left of the birds except bloodstains and feathers which are everywhere. In the corner, slumped on the ground, lies the predator, curled up and snoring.

For a moment, it looks to Helena like a bear. Only it doesn't have fur and it's way too thin. Its skin is dark, and it's not wearing any clothes. Its head is hidden under the arm, and it's only when she sees the six-fingered hand that the truth finally hits home.

She's looking at one of the infected people. Someone who's way farther into the transformation than the woman who attacked her at BESTSELLER.

She recoils as the person—if that's still the right word—stirs and gives off a grunt, as though sensing her standing there.

Helena pulls to the side and out of view. She spins around and is about to run to the cabin. But at the last possible second, she thinks better of it. Running across the grass would be suicide. The thing in the henhouse would catch up with her in a heartbeat—she can already hear it getting to its feet.

Instead, Helena slips around the corner of the henhouse.

And hardly is she out of sight before the monster comes bursting out.

Helena squeezes her lips together and clenches both fists. She hears the thing utter some noises which aren't remotely human. And then the sound of fast, heavy footsteps running for the house.

Helena forces herself to peek around the corner. She sees the figure stop in front of the cabin door. The monster is much bigger now that it's standing erect—its frame looks less like a human and more like a giant spider that's lost half its legs. It whips its bald head around to stare at the truck, and with a shriek it runs and rips off the driver's side door like the vehicle was made of LEGOs. It bends over and sticks its entire upper body inside the car.

Go, a thought urges Helena. *This is your only chance. If you don't make it inside now, it'll find you and kill you.*

So, she sprints for the front door. As soon as she does, she's completely exposed; the monster could pull out of the car any second to see her.

It's only ten yards or so, but it feels like a mile.

She reaches the door. Through a red haze, she sees her hands both going for the key. She turns it. It moves only reluctantly—or maybe it's the muscles in her arm that are cramping up. Behind her, she can hear the monster rummage through the truck, grunting and whining.

Finally, the key turns all the way, and the lock snaps open. The sound is like a gunshot. It makes the sounds from the monster stop at once.

Helena opens the door, her body moving through quicksand, her heart feeling like it's about to burst through her ribcage, her eyesight flickering. She steps inside and turns around in slow motion to see the monster pull back out from the truck. Its blank eyes land on her. It gives a screech and lunges for her. Helena slams the door and steps behind it, pressing her back against the wall.

Maybe half a second passes.

In that space of time, several thoughts shoot through her head.

I should've gone straight to the basement.

I should've called Dad.

I shouldn't even have come up here alone.

Helena stares at the rug only a few paces away. Below it is the hatch. But there's no way she'll reach it.

And then the door bursts open with a loud crash, as the monster throws itself at it. The lock all but explodes, and the door comes flying at Helena. She only just manages to shield her head with her arms. Still, the door hits her with enough force to knock the air out of her lungs, and she can't help but give off a wheezing croak.

The monster doesn't seem to hear her. It roars out and runs through the scullery. As the door swings halfway shut again, Helena sees the intruder disappear into the kitchen, obviously assuming that Helena is trying to get as far away from it as possible.

Get moving. Now!

This thought sounds a lot like her mom when she would once in a while demand something of Helena that wasn't negotiable.

Helena knows where the thought wants her to go. She could run back out to the truck and drive off. But even if she made it back out of the driveway and halfway down the hill, the monster would no doubt notice the truck missing and take up pursuit. And it would catch her.

So, there's really only one place to go.

Helena staggers to the rug, once again feeling like she can't move her arms or legs properly but has to force them to cooperate. As she hears the monster scream—it sounds like it's already reached the living room now—she kneels down and pulls the rug aside. The hatch is still there, the lock too, resting in a small recess her dad had carved into the wooden floor, and it looks exactly like she remembers it from over ten years ago. The hatch isn't easy to see, because it's blending in with the floorboards.

Helena takes the padlock with buzzing fingers, turns it over and sees the digits. And as she's about to dial the combination, she realizes to her horror she can't recall the numbers.

She knows it's her birthday.

She just can't remember what day that is.

Jesus, come on ... What's the date? When's your damn birthday?

She can hear the monster smash things in the living room. The sounds make her thought process block even more.

Come on ... come on, damnit!

She closes her eyes and focuses all her energy on bringing up a memory, anything that'll help her. She sees a scene from a party. It's her seventh or eighth birthday. They're out on the lawn. Under the beech tree. Her mom is reading a book in the hammock. Her dad is lighting up the barbecue. Helena is playing with the gift she unwrapped earlier, a plastic suitcase full of hairdresser stuff. The sound of flies buzzing, birds singing.

It's warm. It's summer. School is out. It's ...

July.

July 24th.

Helena opens her eyes, and the memory disappears like smoke. She starts dialing the numbers.

She's managed the first two when she realizes the cabin has fallen quiet. Her throat closes up. She turns her head and glances towards the kitchen. She can't see anything in the darkness. Listening intently, she hears the floorboard creak somewhere.

It's listening.

Helena focuses on the padlock. Getting the last two digits right, it snaps open. She takes it off as quietly as she can, finding that her hands are a bit more cooperative now. She grabs the edge of the hatch and tries to lift it, but it doesn't give way.

Oh, no ... it's locked from the inside, too ...

But that doesn't make sense. She tries again, lifting harder, and this time, the hatch comes up off the floor. It's a lot heavier than she expected. As she gets it up halfway, she sees why: it's almost two inches thick, and it seems to be made of steel. On the underside are a handle and three thick sliding bolts.

She glances down and sees a ladder leading into a darkness that's even thicker than the one she's currently sitting in. She'll need to be careful, or—

Another creaking floorboard, this one a lot closer.

Helena whips her head around.

And there she sees it. Standing in the opening to the kitchen. Only ten steps away. Seeing it inside, it seems even taller; it's hunched over so as to not bump its bald head. The eyes bore into hers, pinning her in place, and the mouth splits open into a wide grin, revealing rows of razor-sharp teeth.

They react at the exact same time.

The monster lurches forward with a roar.

Helena throws herself headfirst down the opening to the basement.

The hatch slams against her back, shoving her hard forward, before it crashes shut. Helena grabs for the rungs of the ladder, but she doesn't manage to catch any of them. Instead, she knocks her chin on one of them, causing her teeth to clatter with a sickening, painful clack. Then she lands on a hard floor and almost collapses. Ignoring the pain from her mouth, she immediately finds the ladder and climbs back up. The image of the sliding bolts is still in her mind, and she reaches up a hand, feeling for them. She finds the hatch, but before she can locate any of the sliding locks, a crack appears.

"*No!*" Helena screams out as she sees four thin, long fingers squeeze in and start to lift the hatch.

She instinctively grabs the handle with both hands and steps off the ladder, pulling the hatch down with all her weight.

As strong as the monster is, it clearly didn't expect such a hard pull of resistance, and the hatch slams shut, cutting off all four fingers.

The monster screams out—the sound is dampened considerably by the thick hatch—and Helena wastes no time in finding the sliding bolts and slamming all three of them locked.

She then climbs down from the ladder, feeling solid ground under her shoes, and she just stands there in the darkness for several minutes, listening to the roars and whines and screams from the monster above as it claws and hammers away at the hatch.

It doesn't seem to give way.

At least not right away.

I made it. For now.

Swallowing hard to force her heart back down her throat, Helena starts searching for a light.

33

VERONICA

SHE SWALLOWS TWO MORE morphine pills and washes them down with a mouthful of lukewarm coffee from the old guy's thermo flask. But the pain in her leg never really settles, nor does the dizziness go away.

She's alternating between hot and cold flashes. Blinking away drops of sweat, she strains to see the road ahead clearly, while darting nervous looks at Molly.

The girl, unlike Veronica, seems to be feeling perfectly fine. At least she's not in pain or discomfort. She does seem restless, though. Her breathing is a little too fast, and she keeps wringing her hands in her lap. Her fingers already look a bit too long, and Veronica is also pretty sure the girl has grown a few inches.

They've entered back into town. Veronica wants to run every red light she meets, but she needs to drive carefully. If they get pulled over by the cops, there's no way Molly will get any help. The clinic is only five minutes away.

Almost there. Just focus. Don't pass out. You've got this.

She realizes she's using the same affirmations for when she's running longer distances and exhaustion is setting in. Had she not been an experienced endurance runner, she would have probably not been able to push past the pain and fatigue like she is.

Molly grunts.

"What?" Veronica asks alarmed, looking at her. "What is it?"

Molly's hand goes to her mouth, and for a second it looks like she's about to puke. Instead, she picks something out of her mouth and holds it between two thin fingers. It's a molar. She glances sideways at Veronica. Veronica doesn't know what to say. Molly rolls down the window and throws out the tooth.

As they drive on, Veronica notices how the girl keeps running her tongue across her front teeth under her lips.

How long? How long before she turns completely? How long before she lunges at me and bites open my throat?

She doesn't know the answer. Molly is clearly past the sickness stage and has begun transforming. Leo, at this stage, had already taken off into the night to go hunting for human flesh. How come Molly has managed to keep these predatorial urges under control, Veronica has no idea. But she suspects the balance can shift any moment.

They finally reach the clinic.

Veronica parks in one of the handicap spots right by the front door. She opens the glove compartment and finds a pair of sunglasses. "Here," she says, handing them to Molly. "Put these on."

The girl takes the glasses with a wondering look, but puts them on without protesting. Veronica gets out, bringing the lamp pole. It's almost dark by now. An old, frail-looking woman is standing next to the glass doors, leaning on a crutch, smoking a cigarette. She's wearing hospital clothes underneath a heavy jacket.

"Jeez," she says as Veronica comes limping towards the door. "Why didn't you call an ambulance?"

Veronica looks at her. "I need your crutch."

The woman grins. "Yeah, I bet you do."

"No, give it to me," Veronica says, hopping closer. "You go get a new one."

The woman frowns and tightens her grip as Veronica tries to grab the crutch. "Look, I understand you're injured, but I just had surgery, and—"

"Gimme the fucking crutch," Veronica snarls, grabbing for it.

But the woman holds it out of reach and steps away—she's clearly perfectly able to walk. "No. It's mine!"

Before Veronica can do anything, Molly sweeps in from the side and grabs the crutch. The woman is about to protest when Molly takes off the sunglasses and sneers at her. "Let go," she says, her voice now clearly distorted.

The woman lets go of the crutch like it's suddenly red hot. She staggers backwards and drops her cigarette. "Jeez ... oh, jeez ... what the hell ... what the hell's wrong with you?"

Molly hands Veronica the crutch, and she's grateful to lean on something that doesn't hurt her armpit. "Come on," she says to Molly.

The girl sends the woman one last mean look, then puts the sunglasses back on and follows Veronica. As they enter the clinic, Veronica can't help but notice how Molly's gait has become more bopping. Her legs are longer, evident by the fact that her pants are two inches too short. They're the same height now, and soon Molly will be taller than her.

The entrance hall is warm and almost empty save for an orderly pushing a bed across the floor and two women behind the counter.

One of them notices Veronica right away and gets up. "Goodness, what happened to you?"

"I was in an accident," Veronica says simply. "I need to see Luna Poulsen."

"Listen, we're not that kind of hospital," the woman informs her. "We don't have an ER. I can call you an ambu—"

"No, I need to see Luna Poulsen," Veronica repeats. Reaching the counter, she leans on it, breathing heavily. "She works here. She's a friend of mine."

The woman, confused, looks at her colleague. The other woman is older and apparently has more seniority, because she takes over. "I'm afraid is doesn't work like that. For one thing, you can't just walk in an expect to see a doctor. And for another—"

"Fine, I'll call her up myself ..." Veronica fumbles out her phone.

"For another," the woman goes on, "Doctor Poulsen isn't working tonight."

Veronica stops and puts her phone back. "Fuck. Okay. Listen ... we just need to see a doctor. Any doctor. Please, it's important."

The front doors open, and the old woman comes into the building. "Something's wrong with her!" she screeches, pointing at Molly. "She's not ... she looks all ... wrong!"

Both women behind the counter obviously think she's referring to Veronica.

"Look, I can tell you're badly hurt," the woman says, picking up a phone. "And I'll get someone here who can make sure you get the proper help. But I'm sure they'll say the same thing: That they'll need to transfer you to a hospital."

"Just call a doctor," Veronica mutters, closing her eyes as the room spins around itself for a moment. She can sense Molly standing right behind her, impatiently shifting her weight back and forth.

"I'm telling you, something's wrong with her!" the woman cries out. "You should call the police or something. She stole my crutch, too!"

The younger of the receptionists comes around the counter and goes to the old lady, telling her to calm down.

Within thirty seconds, a young, bald doctor comes striding towards Veronica. "What's the problem?" he asks.

"This young woman—"

"I'm hurt," Veronica tells him. "My leg …"

The doctor looks briefly at the bloody bandage, then he looks back at Veronica's face, studying her. "She's in shock," he concludes. "Call an ambulance."

"No," Veronica mutters. "I just need to talk to you …"

"Call an ambulance now," the doctor tells the woman behind the counter, taking Veronica's arm. "Tell them I'll be in H5 with her when they get here."

"Thank you," Veronica whispers, almost bursting into tears from exhaustion and relief. "Come along, Molly …"

Molly follows suit. Behind them, the old woman is still yelling.

34

HELENA

SHE USES THE LIGHT from her phone to scan the wall for a switch. She doesn't find one.

From up above, the monster clearly isn't intent on giving up. It must be either punching or stomping the hatch, producing deep, rhythmical bangs which reverberate inside the basement like distant claps of thunder.

How long will it hold?

Helena initially thought she'd bought herself hours, but judging by the sound of the pounding, she's not so sure the hatch will hold for more than minutes. She's felt how strong the transformed people are, and even a steel door might not be enough to hold the person up there out for long.

"Where's the damn light, Dad?"

The darkness swallows up her voice, giving her no answer. She turns over her phone and tries to call him up. It tells her NO SERVICE. She tries that thing they always do in the movies, raising the phone over her head. It doesn't produce even a single signal bar.

"Damnit!"

It must be the basement that's somehow screwing the signal.

The bangs seem to be growing louder. In between, she can hear grunts and groans, and something else, something closer by. It's a soft drizzling. She points the light at the ladder and sees dust falling like snow. Pulverized concrete.

God. It's breaking through.

Helena gives up finding the light. Instead, she ventures into the basement, following the wall. The basement is larger than she thought. She sees the beds her dad told her about—they look more like military cots—a table, a couple of chairs, two large fridges which seem to be on, and a few other pieces of furniture. She doesn't pay them much attention. What she's looking for is either a way to contact her dad—some kind of radio or phone that can make a call despite the concrete walls—or something to defend herself with.

She finds the latter.

On the far wall is mounted a steel cabinet almost as tall as Helena. The door and the sides are both perforated with small, round holes, making her able to see the guns and dozens of metal boxes. They're all marked with stickers with names like ".40 S&W," "9mm," "7.62 NATO," and "12 ga." None of them mean anything to her. She tries to open the door, but finds another combination padlock, this one smaller. She tries the same four digits, but it doesn't open. Then she tries Mom's birthday. No luck. Dad's. Nope.

"Fuck!" she hisses, batting away a lock of hair that keeps getting in her eyes. "What's the code, Dad?"

The thuds from above have changed. Instead of the monster slowing down, as you would expect once exhaustion set in, it seems to be pounding away faster and harder. The sounds are more rattly now, as though the hatch isn't lying snug in the frame anymore, but starting to become loose. Or maybe the hinges are giving way.

Helena can't think of any other person in her dad's life whose birthday he might have used for the code. But then again, maybe it's not a birthday at all, or maybe …

"Maybe it's not a person," Helena mutters, dialing 0212—Buddy's birthday.

The padlock opens with a click.

"Yes!"

She rips open the door and stares at all the firearms for a second. There are two pistols, and she chooses the newer-looking one. It's a lot heavier than it looks. She assumes it doesn't have any bullets in it—this seems to be confirmed by the hole she sees at the butt end of the handle, which is where she assumes the magazine goes. And there are plenty of magazines, neatly stacked in an open container—the problem is, none of them have bullets in them, which means she'll need to load them first.

She puts the phone on one of the shelves and starts going through the boxes of ammo. The first two both have individual bullets that look too big—she's fairly certain they're for rifles or shotguns. The bullets in the third box, the one marked "9 mm," look a lot more fitting in size. She takes out one and tries to put it in, but it falls to the floor.

She looks at the gun in her hand, turning it over, trying to pull back the top part which she's seen people do in the movies. And she actually succeeds, revealing a small space that she's pretty certain is called the chamber. Maybe she can just put the bullet right in there?

She crouches down and strains her eyes to see the bullet she dropped. It must have rolled away because she can't find it.

Suddenly, the hatch gives way.

The sound of the busted metal plate clanging to the floor is deafening. Helena sees a faint light coming down through a cloud of dust. A shadow moves up above, and the monster exclaims something akin to a victory cry.

Helena's heart almost stops. She's not ready. She's completely exposed again, and this time, there's nowhere to run.

She's about to get up when she sees it. Right in front of her face. Attached to the underside of the cabinet. A single magazine. This one has bullets in it. Helena reaches out and takes it. She tries to put it in, and it slides up the gun with ease. As it clicks into place, Helena feels a wild elation.

She gets to her feet as the monster comes plunging down the opening, landing gracefully on top of the bent hatch. It scans the basement, apparently able to see without trouble in the dark, and the awful, white eyes fix on Helena.

She aims the gun at it, clutching it with both hands, stretching her arms like she's seen people do on television. She doesn't wait for the monster to approach her, but pulls the trigger right away. She doesn't really expect the gun to fire. She expects there's a safety of some kind. But either it's already off, or there isn't one. Because the gun fires all right.

There's a brief, blinding flash, and something punches against her eardrums. The recoil is much more violent than she thought, causing her elbows to bend, and she almost drops the gun. But she manages to keep hold of it, and blinks and sees the silhouette of the monster still standing. She can't tell if it's growling or screaming at her, because her hearing is nothing more than a buzz, but it clearly isn't dead, so Helena fires the gun again, and again, and again, biting down hard while she keeps squeezing the trigger.

She doesn't count how many times she fires. At one point, she feels something whiz by her cheek, almost grazing her ear. Then, suddenly, the trigger feels lose, and the gun no longer fires when she presses it.

Helena stares at the monster—seeing to her horror how it's still standing.

Oh, no. I missed with every shot ...

But then the figure leans to the side. It grabs hold of the ladder with one hand, as though wanting to support itself. Then its knees give way as it keels over and slumps to the floor.

35

VERONICA

THE DOCTOR BRINGS THEM into some kind of examination room. He helps Veronica to sit on the treatment couch and absentmindedly tells Molly to take a seat on the chair by the wall. The girl does as she's told, still wearing her sunglasses.

Then the doctor goes to a cupboard and begins putting on gloves. "Can you take off your jacket?" he asks, not turning around. "Or do you need me to help you?"

Instead of unzipping her jacket, Veronica unwraps the blanket and takes the gun. She aims it at the doctor, taking a deep breath to steady herself. "I'm very sorry to do this to you," she says.

Something in her tone makes the doctor turn around. He freezes. Looks from Veronica to the gun and back again. Then he slowly raises both hands—one of them with a glove on. "There's no need for that. I'll treat you as best I can until the—"

"I'm not here for treatment."

He shakes his head and gives a nervous little laugh. "Well, we've got no money here. It's a health clinic. We only—"

"Shut up, please. It's her." She nods at Molly. "I need you to fix her."

The doctor, looking even more perplexed, glances briefly at the girl. "What ...? Why would you—"

"Lock the door first," Veronica tells him. "Lock it. Now."

The doctor hesitates briefly.

"Please don't test me," Veronica sighs. "I'm so damn tired, and I've been through a lot these past twenty-four hours. Believe me, I will pull the trigger if I have to." She's surprised to find that she means it.

The guy can evidently tell too that she's serious, because he swallows, then goes and turns the lock.

"Please put down the gun," he says as he turns back around. "I'll cooperate. There's no need for threats."

"You've got a mask in there?" Veronica asks, nodding at the cupboard. "Something to cover your mouth?"

He frowns. "Yes."

"Put it on, then."

"You want *me* to ...?"

"Yes, you. Go on."

He goes and puts on a mask.

"And the other glove," Veronica instructs.

He's still holding it, so he puts it on.

"Okay," Veronica says, shivering. "I need to tell you something. If you freak out and try to leave ..." She bobs the gun, implying that she'll fire it. "We were just on the Isle of Heir."

She waits to see if he gets it. The doctor frowns, clearly not following.

"That virus or infection or whatever ... the one they're talking about ... what was it they called it?" She racks her brain, trying to remember what the medic said.

"Nigrumycosis?" the doctor asks, his forehead now full of creases.

"Yes! Exactly. A lot of people on the island got it. And ... Molly did too."

They both look at the girl who's glancing back and forth at them. Veronica is struck by how awkward she looks. Like an overgrown teenager at a parents-teacher meeting who's gotten herself into trouble. The ridiculous sunglasses make it even more absurd.

"You mean to tell me …?" The doctor swallows again. He takes a step back. It looks more like a reflex than an attempt to run away.

"Stay where you are," Veronica tells him. "I'm pretty sure it only infects through touch, so don't worry."

"Are you absolutely sure she's got it?" he asks.

Veronica looks at the girl. "Take off your glasses, Molly."

Molly takes them off.

"Jesus Christ almighty," the doctor breathes. It looks like he really wants to run away, but to his credit, he stays put.

"Take five seconds to compute," Veronica tells him. "Then fix her."

He stares at her. "What do you mean?"

"I mean, do whatever you can to make her normal again."

"Are you insane?" He scoffs and gestures at Molly with both hands. "Look at her! She's starting to transform! There's nothing anyone can do for her!"

"Don't speak like that," Veronica says through gritted teeth. "I didn't come all this way to—"

"I'm sorry, but it's the truth," the doctor says. "As much as I want to help her, there's absolutely nothing I can do."

"You didn't even look at her!" Veronica says, raising her voice. "You haven't … I don't know, run any tests or whatever. Try something, for God's sake!"

"Try something?" the guy repeats. "This isn't like cooking. I can't just throw something in a pot and see what happens."

"Yes, you can. Or I swear to God, I'll blow your fucking head off." She takes aim. She's trembling so badly now, she's not sure she'll hit him, even at this close range.

"Listen, listen," he says, holding out his gloved palms. "Okay, here's the deal. I can give her something. I can give her whatever you want. Antibiotics, antifungal, whatever you want. Here, let me show you …" He strides back to the cupboard, opens the door and reveals rows full of bottles, glass, packages. "We've got it all here. We could even put her through radiation. But I'm telling you, none of it will do her any good." He takes a step closer to Veronica—not in a threatening way, just to make his case clearer—and he puts emphasis on every word. "This isn't a regular disease. It's not even from this planet."

Molly gives off a grunt and moves on the chair, as though she suddenly becomes upset.

Veronica frowns. "What are you talking about?"

"I assume you haven't been following," the doctor goes on. "But they're looking into one of the early victim's DNA, and it's not from around here. This spore, it's changing people. It's rewriting their code." He points at Molly but keeps looking at Veronica. "I'm sorry to tell you this so bluntly, but your girl …" He shakes his head hard. "She's no longer human."

At this, Molly lunges off the chair with a screeching roar.

"*No!*" Veronica screams as she crosses the room, but Molly doesn't hear her.

The doctor veers back and roars out through the mask. Molly jumps him like she did the old guy, only she's noticeably bigger now, and the doctor clearly knows some kind of self-defense, because he grabs her arms, turns around and uses her own speed to send her crashing into the wall. Molly is rattled but not knocked out. She shakes her head and turns around to face the doctor. As she does, she reminds Veronica very much of Leo. And in a flash, it finally dawns on her tired brain that this was a big mistake. That it really is too late. That she should've never come here.

"Stop, Molly!" she shouts, not expecting the girl to listen. And she doesn't. She gives off a snarl and is about to jump the doctor again, when he suddenly steps forward and plunges something into her neck.

Veronica screams out as he steps back, afraid that she'll see a knife or scalpel or something else deadly sticking out from Molly's neck. What she sees is a syringe. Molly grabs it, yanks it out, looks at it, and throws it aside. Then she snarls and goes for the doctor again. But he's run to the other side of the room and picked up the chair Molly was sitting on before. Holding it up like a lion tamer, he stares intently at Molly.

The girl walks across the floor, but as she does, one of her legs suddenly buckle. She goes down on one knee with a grunt. Breathing heavily, she tries to get back up, but instead she collapses onto her stomach. Turning her head sideways, her blank eyes look up at Veronica, and just before Molly passes out, Veronica swears she sees the girl in there for the last time.

36

HELENA

SHE STANDS FOR A long moment nailed to the spot in the darkness of the basement. Her wrists and elbows are aching from the recoil. Her head is thrumming. Her mouth is dry.

The monster is slumped to the floor, leaning against the lower rung of the ladder. Amazingly, it's still breathing; even from over here, Helena can tell its ribcage is expanding and contracting.

Get the hell out.

Mom's voice again.

She considers for a brief moment trying to refill the gun and finish the job. But then the monster begins stirring, and Helena takes her late mother's advice. Dropping the gun, she has just enough presence of mind to bring her phone with her as she goes back towards the ladder.

Her hearing is still not working right, but she can make out pitiful noises from the monster on the floor. Its breath is rattly, and it gives off a screechy whimper. Blood is dripping from several puncture wounds, one of them in the lower part of the neck. It coughs and spits out a cascade of black, foamy saliva.

If Helena didn't know any better, she would've thought the creature was dying for sure. That it had seconds left to live.

But even as she's staring at it, she sees a wound on its upper arm close up and disappear.

It can do the same as Dad. Only a lot faster.

Apparently, the monster hasn't noticed Helena standing right next to it. So she carefully steps over it and places her foot on the ladder. It's not easy because the creature is still leaning against it, but she manages to step up without touching it. For a second, Helena is hanging right above its head. If it looks up, it'll see her.

But the monster doesn't look up. It's still too hurt from the gunshots.

Helena scales the ladder as quickly and quietly as she can. For every step, she expects a strong hand will grab her ankle, just like it almost always happens in horror movies. She feels almost convinced she'll be dragged back down and killed and that'll be the end of it.

But no hand grabs her.

As she climbs through the opening—which is now all rugged at the edges—she hears the monster utter a screech. Getting to her feet, she can't help but glance back down. What she sees makes the hairs on her arms all stand on end.

The monster is glaring up at her. It's only got one eye left—the other is a gaping, black hole. The bullet seems to have caught the outer edge of the eye socket and punctured the eyeball on its way, blowing out the temple. Yet the monster is clearly still cognizant, because at the sight of her peering back down at it, its mouth contorts into a hateful snarl, and it grabs for the ladder, pulling itself up.

Helena should run, but instead, she steps sideways to the washer, and before she even knows what she's going to do, she has grabbed the clay pot that she made for Mom's birthday several years ago, and which Dad still uses to keep the soap tablets. Helena turns around, raising the pot over her head just as the monster reaches the top of the ladder. She throws down the pot as hard as she can, slamming it squarely into the top of the monster's skull. It explodes and sends soap bars in every direction. The monster gives a grunt, but, to Helena's surprise, manages to cling on to the ladder.

She kicks it on the chin, causing it to give a roar of anger, and as she's about to kick it again, it reaches out an arm to grab her leg. Helena pulls away and runs for the door. She has no options left. She can only make a dash for the truck and hope to get away. It's a bad plan, but it's all she's got.

Slamming the front door after her, she hears it open again even before she reaches the truck. She doesn't look back, but simply throws herself in behind the wheel. She pushes down the clutch, grabs the key, turns it, and the engine coughs to life. Looking out the windscreen, she sees the monster coming for the car. It doesn't walk right; it's hunched over, clutching its side, as though still hurt. And for a split second, Helena thinks this means she'll make it.

Then she grabs for the stick to put the car in reverse, but her hand finds nothing. Looking down in confusion, she sees the gear lever all bent to the side. In a flash, she sees the monster rummage wildly through the truck.

Oh, no ... it broke it.

She grabs the lever anyway and tries to force it into reverse, but the gearbox only gives off a nasty, crunching sound.

"No! No!"

She reaches for the door, wanting to close it, before remembering the monster tore it off and flung it away—but then ...

Then the creature is suddenly gone.

Helena stares in the direction where she saw it only moments ago. Nothing's there. Whipping her head around, she checks all around the idling truck. She can't see the creature anywhere.

Holding her breath, she waits for it to pop up and attack the car.

But it doesn't.

Nothing happens for several seconds.

What the hell? Where'd it go?

37

VERONICA

"What ... what did you give her?"

The doctor slowly puts the chair back down, not taking his eyes off Molly. "Something that'll keep her sleeping for a while," he says. "We need to get out of here. Before we catch the—"

"I'm not going anywhere," Veronica cuts him off.

He looks at her leg. "Your wound. It's clearly infected. You need treatment right away."

"You can leave now," she murmurs, looking at Molly. "Thanks for your help."

He hesitates. "Come with me, please." He sounds almost kind now. "Let me treat you. You're septic, but I see no signs of the spore on you. It might not be too late to save your life."

"Believe me," she says in a toneless voice, "it's way too late. Go, please."

He sends her one last look, seemingly debating whether to keep arguing the point. Then he simply turns, goes to the door, unlocks it and steps outside. Veronica gets up with a wince, limps to the door and relocks it.

She looks down at Molly. She's breathing in short, gaspy breaths. She looks like she's sleeping.

A red flashing light goes by the window. The glass is not see-through for privacy reasons, but it's unmistakably a police light she just saw.

Doesn't matter if they arrest me. I'll be dead within a few hours anyway.

But the girl. She doesn't want Molly to end up in the authorities' custody. God knows what they'll do to her.

A loud banging on the door makes Veronica jump.

"*Hello?*" a gruff male voice calls from the other side. "*Can you hear me in there?*"

Veronica is suddenly uncertain what to do. She had resigned herself to pulling the trigger and ending Molly's misery. But now ... now there might be another way.

She goes to the window and opens it. Peeking outside, she sees the parking lot. Two cop cars are parked by the front door along with an ambulance, the lights still going, although all three vehicles appear to be empty. Closer to the window is the SUV.

There comes another bang from the door. "*Please open the door, or we'll have to kick it in!*"

Veronica makes her decision.

38

HELENA

HELENA KNOWS THE DANGER isn't over. She knows it's a trick. But what she doesn't understand is, what's the point? Why would the monster suddenly try and play some ploy when it was seconds away from getting at her?

Stretching her neck, she checks the ground around the truck. She can't see anything. Could it have dived down and crawled under the truck? As skinny as it was, Helena still doubts the boney frame of the monster could fit below the undercarriage.

And again ... why would it go through the trouble of hiding?

Helena looks farther out into the darkness. Scanning the lawn, the driveway, the meadow leading to the forest. No sign of the monster.

A frail hope starts allowing her heart to unclench just a bit.

Did it ... did it really just ... take off?

Surely, it wouldn't suddenly decide she wasn't worth the trouble. Unless something scared it off. Or maybe ... maybe it sensed something else? Something more appealing?

Helena doesn't like the situation one bit. She tries again to put the truck in gear, but it doesn't work. Instead, she takes out her phone and calls up Dad.

Just as she puts the phone against her ear, she catches a movement in the side mirror. A big figure comes into view as it turns into the driveway—a figure she knows well, despite some recent alterations. Next to it is another figure, one with four legs but equally familiar.

"Dad!" Helena gasps, ending the call. "Dad! Oh, God ..."

She tries to open the door, then remembers it's locked. She pulls the lock, but it doesn't slide back up easily—apparently, it took a hit too while the monster went through the car. Either that, or it just hasn't been used for a long time.

"Dad!" Helena shouts, slamming the window as he approaches the car from behind. "Dad, I'm in here!"

He stops by the driver's door and bends over to look in at her. "Hey, honey. Something wrong?"

"Yes!" she cries out, almost bursting into tears. "I can't ... I can't get this open ..."

"No, it's a little quirky," her dad says. "You need to jiggle it. No, not like that. From side to side."

Helena can barely focus on what he's saying. She wants to get out, wants to tell him what happened, wants to warn him that they might all be in danger. Buddy slinks around the truck, sniffing eagerly, whimpering. Whether the dog can smell her and is eager to greet her, or whether it smells the monster and feels anxious, Helena can't really tell.

"Dad!" she says, giving up on the lock. "Dad, you need to listen to me ..."

"It's not that hard," Dad says, pointing at the lock. "Just move it a little, and then—"

"No, Dad!" she almost screams. "Listen! There was an alien. It ... it attacked me ..."

Dad's eyes widen. "What? When?"

"Just now!"

"Jesus," he breathes, looking her up and down. "Are you okay?" He instinctively grabs the door, even though he knows it's locked, and gives it a yank that's hard enough to cause the truck to sway. "Damnit!"

"I'm okay, I'm not hurt," Helena tells him. "But it could still—"

"Hold on, sweetie." He jogs around the front of the car. For a moment, he blocks the headlights, which are pointing at the cabin. When the still-open front door appears a split-second later, the alien is standing there, glaring at them.

"Dad! Daaad!" Helena screams. She yanks the door, still to no avail. She points at the cabin and keeps screaming for her dad.

He opens the passenger door and leans into the car. "What is it?" he demands, looking around the inside of the car, as though expecting something dangerous in here. "What's wrong, swe—"

"It's right there, Dad!" Helena screams, pointing at the cabin. "It's coming! Look out!"

Her dad retracts his upper body and turns towards the cabin. Helena looks in that direction too. Now, the front door is empty. The monster is nowhere in sight.

"Are you sure you saw something?" her dad asks, glancing in at her again.

"Yes! It was right there!"

As though confirming her claim, Buddy starts barking shrilly. Helena can't see the dog, but it sounds like he's somewhere behind the truck. Her dad swirls around. "Buddy? What is it?"

The monster reappears suddenly. Popping up from behind, it grabs her dad before Helena has time to warn him.

It wraps both arms around his chest, buries its teeth in his neck, and wrestles him to the ground. Helena hears her father groan in pain before the sound is drowned out by Buddy's desperate bark as the dog comes racing around the truck and lunges at the creature's back.

Helena can't really see what's going on, but she can hear the monster screech, hear Buddy bark, hear her dad croak. Then there's a loud thud, and Buddy flies through the air, landing on the ground with a whimper. He tries to get up but can't.

Helena finds herself climbing over the broken gear lever and is about to exit the truck through the open passenger door, when her dad, still with the monster clinging to his back like a living turtle shield, bursts into the door hard enough for one of the hinges to break.

Helena screams and pulls back inside the truck.

Her dad tries to get the alien off, tries to throw it over his shoulder, tries to reach its head, he even slams it into the side of the truck, causing two of the wheels to lift a few inches off the ground and the window to shatter.

But the monster is clinging on like a lion to a gazelle. As they turn around, Helena sees to her horror a fountain of blood sprinkle from her dad's neck where the alien is still biting down hard. His face is turning blue, and she realizes the alien is suffocating him.

She tumbles out of the car and begins kicking away at the monster's back. It doesn't even seem to notice. She grabs its arm and tries to peel it free. No use. Her dad does one last move, rolling over, almost knocking Helena to the ground. The alien holds on, and even though it ends up at the bottom, her dad doesn't manage to break free. Now he's lying on his back, and he suddenly seems unable to fight back. His eyes are bulging out their sockets, staring up at the dark sky.

"*Daaad!*" Helena hears herself scream.

She has no idea what to do. There's nothing she *can* do. The monster is way too strong. If only she had the gun, but not only is it still in the basement, it's also got no bullets left, and finding and loading it would take her several minutes. By then, her dad will be dead.

All she can do is stand here, watching helplessly as the monster kills her dad.

39

VERONICA

She keeps checking the rearview mirror until she's out of town.

No police cars are following her.

How she got away clean, she's still not sure. And how she got Molly out through the window, that's an even bigger mystery.

All Veronica knows is, it cost her a lot of energy—energy she doesn't have. Weirdly, the wound doesn't hurt as badly anymore. Instead, her entire leg has become mostly numb.

She's focusing on the road, straining to stay awake. It's completely dark outside now, and she's driving way too fast through the open landscape. But at least no other cars are out, so she only risks running into a deer or sliding off the frozen road.

Hornstedt is only ten minutes out, when there suddenly comes a grunt from the backseat.

Veronica looks up into the mirror. "You awake?"

Molly comes into view as she sits up. Her eyes are swimming, but they immediately find Veronica's in the mirror, and her expression turns hateful.

"I'm sorry," Veronica tells her. "I know it's not pleasant, but ... I had to do it."

Molly says something, but it's muffled by the tape covering the lower part of her face. Molly's forearms are also taped together behind her back, as are her shins. Had Veronica not taken the time to tape her up using the roll of duct tape from the old guy's bag, Molly would probably already have dug into her neck.

She begins groaning as she fights the tape.

"I don't think it's coming off," Veronica informs her. "I used the entire roll."

Molly stops writhing and instead glares at Veronica.

"Are you okay?" Veronica asks her. "How are you feeling?"

She looks at Molly for a reaction.

The girl just shakes her head. As she does, a tuft of her pretty black hair falls off. Molly doesn't seem to notice. Looking at her, Veronica can tell she transformed even faster while she was out. The shape of her skull is all wrong. It's hard to tell because of the tape, but her jawline seems a lot broader and longer, too. Her shoulders are wider and sit higher. And she's a head taller than Veronica now.

"Look," Veronica goes on. "I don't know what to do anymore ..." She shakes her head and sighs. "I should have just stayed home. Or better yet, turned myself in. None of this would've happened ..." She begins crying. It's just as much from exhaustion as regret. She wipes away the tears and looks at Molly again. The girl is sitting completely still, watching her. "I didn't want to leave you at the hospital. I don't think they would have treated you well. And they don't have a cure." She shrugs.

Molly shakes her head slowly and says something.

"I can't understand you."

Molly twists her neck, rolls her head, and then, to Veronica's surprise, she begins gnawing away at the tape from the inside. At first, it looks like a futile attempt. But then Veronica hears ripping noises, and she utters a swear word and quickly pulls over. She grabs the gun from the passenger seat, swirls it around, turning as much as she can, and aims at Molly's chest.

"Please stop, Molly."

But it's too late; most of the tape is already torn. Through the ragged hole, Veronica sees long, pointy teeth that have no resemblance to Molly's. A thin, pink tongue comes snaking out and licks all around the tape, like a snake checking out its surroundings.

"Are you ... are you going to try and hurt me?" Veronica asks, the gun shaking in her hands. Because of the awkward position, she can't hold the weapon properly, and she'll likely drop it if she pulls the trigger, so she'll only get one shot. But at this close range, it ought to be enough—provided she doesn't miss

Molly's tongue disappears back into her mouth, and she smacks her lips behind the tape. Then she says in a voice that's barely human anymore: "Let me go. I'll spare you."

Veronica breathes through her nose. "I wanna help you, Molly. I wanna figure out a way to—"

"No help," Molly says, shaking her head.

"Why not?" Veronica asks, wanting to cry again. She fears the answer, but she asks the question anyway. "Is it ... is it too late?"

Molly cocks her head and says in a tone that's almost overbearing. "Veronica. Too late ten hours ago."

Veronica squeezes her lips together hard as tears once again fill her eyes. "Fuck," she mutters. "Fuck, fuck, *fuck*."

And she finally allows the awful truth to enter her mind. It's been there, the entire time. Ever since she first saw the black stuff growing on Molly. Part of her knew already then that there was no happy ending. That it would end like this no matter what she did or how long she denied it.

And now it's here. And Veronica can no longer pretend there's any hope.

As she sobs, Molly's eyes are pinned on her. Whatever sedative was in her system has clearly gone completely now. The girl—who isn't a girl any longer, no more than Veronica is a mermaid—stares fixedly at her, awaiting Veronica's decision. There's something predatorial over her face. It's like being eyed by a hungry tiger. Veronica feels nauseous.

"This is all my fault," she weeps. "I fucked up. And now everyone's dead."

Molly's mouth opens and closes. As though she's testing her jaw muscles. "It's okay," she says with her new voice. She's trying to sound like her old self, speaking softly, but Veronica can tell it's mock empathy. There's no trace of the sweet girl left, only an impostor. "Let me go, Veronica."

Veronica sniffs. "If I let you go ... what will you do?"

"Leave," Molly says right away. She glances sideways, out into the darkness, as though she's genuinely longing to run off and disappear.

"But ... will you kill anyone?"

The girl opens and shuts her mouth once more. "Noo," she says, drawing out the word, making it sound like a promise.

Veronica blinks away the tears and nods. "Okay." She swallows. "I'm going to let you go, Molly. Just ... gimme a second, okay?"

Molly's nostrils flare. She looks like it's all she can do to stay seated.

Veronica shakes her head. "Before I let you go, there's something I wanna say. I need you to know how sorry I am about all this. I never meant for any of this to happen. I know you can't forgive me, but …"

"Forgive you," Molly says right away. And she pulls up the corners of her mouth as best she can, sending Veronica what's undoubtedly intended as a warm smile. It looks like the grin of a crocodile.

Suddenly, Veronica doesn't feel like crying anymore. "No, I mean … you can't forgive me, because you're not her anymore."

The awful smile turns alert.

"Goodbye, Molly," Veronica says, closing one eye.

Molly explodes off the seat. She doesn't try to get out of the way—if she had simply leaned sideways, Veronica would have likely missed. Instead, the girl lunges forward, opening her mouth with such force that the last of the tape snaps, and the last thing Veronica sees is a way-too-big hole full of teeth coming right at her.

Then she pulls the trigger and blows Molly's head off.

Veronica drops the gun and slumps down into the seat.

She doesn't cry—there's nothing left to cry for. She doesn't feel anything.

She just sits there, in the darkness of the car. Sensing the rumble of the engine. Smelling blood and brain matter. Waiting for death to come. She closes her eyes, hoping to help it along.

But she doesn't die. Her lungs keep breathing, her heart keeps pumping.

"Why?" she asks, opening her eyes again. "What's the point of all this?"

She was dead before the bird even hit her. She was going to die no matter what happened, good ending or bad. She thought her purpose was to save the girl, had clung on to that belief right up until the last moment.

But now, Molly's dead.

"So, what's the point, damnit?" Veronica demands, raising her voice, staring out into the night. "Tell me. Am I supposed to blow my own head off too?"

That doesn't seem like the right answer, but nothing better presents itself. The night is quiet, giving her nothing.

"Okay," Veronica says, taking the gun again. "Okay, I'll do it. At least I can finally—"

As she swings the gun around, the butt hits the dashboard, and a flatscreen lights up. It shows the national news channel. There's a picture of man—it almost looks like a mugshot—in the corner, and Veronica recognizes him. It's the guy from the forest. The one she almost bumped into. The caption reads: "Monster or Messiah?"

A news reporter is talking to the camera with a very serious expression. "... *viral video is being confirmed by several eyewitnesses who claim that Iversen was in fact able to heal the wound on his daughter just by touching it. The incident happened right after a fight with an infected woman. Sources within the police reported that Iversen was helping them track down infected people, even though the official statement from the police is that Iversen is a fugitive and should not be approached if encountered, as he himself is carrying the disease and seems to be mutating ...*"

The picture cuts again to what looks like a handheld camera from a cantina somewhere. There are several cops present, and there's clearly been fighting going on.

"*After the incident,*" the reporter goes on, talking over the footage, "*Iversen took off with his daughter and hasn't been seen since."* They cut back to the reporter. "*Opinions vary about where exactly Iversen stands in all this. Is he a vigilante with godlike powers, trying to stop disaster, or is he simply another infected monster? After his disappearance, some fear he's dead, and along with him, the last hope for mankind. Others feel too much is being read into Iversen's role in the spiraling disaster. Either way, things are quickly escalating, with the latest numbers suggesting there are now more than four hundred confirmed cases of infection. Authorities have issued a nationwide curfew, and—*"

Veronica shuts off the television.

She puts the gun back on the passenger seat.

Images in her memory. The forest. The big guy. She's less than three miles out.

"Thank you," she tells the darkness. "Got it."

She puts the car in drive.

40

HELENA

SHE'S JUST ABOUT TO throw herself at the creature again—she's prepared to claw at it with her nails, even bite it with her teeth if she has to—when a second car suddenly turns into the driveway. Its lights are off, so Helena didn't notice it coming up the road.

It stops abruptly, and even before it's ceased rolling, the door opens and a woman comes tumbling out. She's carrying a gun, limping badly, and even in the dim lighting, Helena can tell she's really sick. This doesn't stop her, though. She goes right up to the fight, aims the gun at the monster's head, and pulls the trigger.

Most of the alien's skull disappears. It never saw the woman coming. Releasing its grip on her father, it slumps to the ground.

Dad rolls onto his hands and knees, coughing and spitting. Blood is dripping from his neck, but it doesn't look as bad as Helena initially thought. Maybe the monster didn't try to rip out her dad's jugular but was simply going for the choke. Or maybe her dad is healing faster this time.

Whatever the case, he's soon able to look around. Seeing Helena, he reaches out a blood-smeared hand. She goes and takes it. "Oh, Dad ... I'm sorry ... I couldn't ... I tried to ..."

"I'm okay," he assures her, his voice hoarse. "Buddy?"

It's only now Helena remembers the dog. "Let me go check." She runs to the place where Buddy landed. He's still lying there, his tail wagging eagerly as she approaches. He's not getting up, though, and Helena immediately sees why: Three long gashes run across the upper part of his hindquarter. His fur is sticky with blood. It's not bad enough that he'll bleed out, but it's clear that he can't stand up.

"Oh, Buddy," she sniffs, crouching down to let him lick away her tears with his warm, wet tongue. "I'm glad you're okay, too."

She goes back to her dad. He's sitting on his butt now, carefully touching the side of his neck. "Damnit, he got me good ..."

"You're bleeding," Helena remarks.

"Yeah, but it's fine. I'm already closing up."

She can see he's right; the tiny puncture wounds are disappearing one after the other, and the blood has almost stopped running.

"What about ...?" He turns his head to look at the woman.

Helena almost forgot about her, too.

She's no longer standing there. Apparently unable to stay on her feet, she's lain down on her side, still holding the gun. Helena goes to her to thank her for saving her dad. But when she sees the woman's face, she can tell she's no longer conscious.

"She fainted," Helena tells her dad. "I think she's very sick. You need to help her, Dad. You need to heal her like you did with me."

Her dad grunts as he gets to his feet. He sways for a second, then finds his balance. "Let's get inside. It's freezing out here."

41

TIM

THE CABIN IS ONLY slightly warmer than the outside.

Helena immediately gets a fire going, and Tim carries first Buddy, then the woman inside. Tim is exhausted and ravenous. He feels like he can barely keep his eyes open. Fighting the alien and then healing his own wounds—his neck is still throbbing with a dull pain whenever he turns his head—it took the last of his strength.

If he's to help Buddy and the woman, he needs to eat.

"Honey," he mutters, slumping down on the couch next to the woman. Buddy is on the floor, carefully licking the bloody cuts on his thigh. "Go grab me something from the fridge, will ya? Anything edible."

Helena nods and goes to the kitchen. She returns a moment later, her arms full. "I couldn't find anything but this …"

"It's fine," Tim says, waving her closer, his mouth watering at the sight of the food.

"But, Dad, it's—"

"I don't care. Gimme."

She puts everything down on the table in front of him, and Tim goes to work. He slurps the mayo out of the plastic bottle, gulping it down. Then he unwraps the cheese and eats half of it in one bite.

"There's a jar of honey in the pantry," he tells Helena between mouthfuls. "And a bag of sugar. Oh, and I think there's half a bottle of Jack."

Helena hesitates only briefly. Then she gets the stuff for him. Tim swallows the honey and licks the inside of the jar. Then he pours the sugar into his mouth, washing it down with swigs of whiskey until the bag and the bottle are both empty. He thumps his chest and lets out a long burb.

"That's better," he murmurs, wiping his mouth with the back of his hand. "I feel reenergized."

"I hope so," Helena remarks, looking at the mess on the table. "You just downed a week's worth of calories."

Tim turns to look at the woman. Her face is pale, her forehead is beady with sweat, and she's trembling. Tim already knew she's infected with something; he noticed a putrid smell when he carried her in here. Carefully pulling up her pant leg, he finds a moist bandage.

"She's septic. I'm not sure I can help her."

"You have to try, Dad."

"I will." He gets to his feet and goes to the dog. "I'll try Buddy first. He's got to be a lot easier."

Buddy shifts a little as Tim kneels and gently places his palm on his leg.

"It's all right, Buddy. Easy now."

The dog licks his hand, then just watches him.

Tim closes his eyes and concentrates. He's got no real idea how it's done. He still doesn't know how he did it to Helena. Only that he was desperate. The process itself wasn't really something he did—it was more like something that happened *through* him.

For a few seconds, nothing happens. Buddy whimpers a little, as though uncertain what's going on. Tim bites down and focuses even harder. He thinks of Buddy. Remembers him as a pup. Hears his first yelps, smells his fur and feels his tiny teeth on his arm from when they used to play-wrestle. Tim isn't sure why all these fond memories pop up, but his palm starts to feel warm and tingly.

It's happening. It's working.

Buddy whimpers again, but this time, it sounds different. As though he's excited.

Then it's over. Tim opens his eyes and lifts his hand. Buddy immediately sniffs the wounds—only they're no longer wounds, but scars, closed and still puffy from the healing process.

Tim rubs his palm, feeling the tingly sensation subside.

"You did it," Helena whispers over his shoulder. She comes around to give Buddy a hug. The dog licks her ear, and, getting to his feet, he slinks around them a few times, as though testing his leg.

"Good boy," Tim tells him, receiving a series of dog kisses under his chin. Then he gets up and turns towards the couch.

"Go on, Dad," Helena urges him as Tim just stands there, looking at the woman. "Now her."

"Yeah," he says, sounding uncertain. "I'll give it a try."

He goes and kneels down by the woman's hips. He's not sure if he needs to remove the bandage, but he doesn't think so, so he leaves it on and just rests his palm on top of it. As he touches it, the woman jolts but doesn't wake up.

"She's in a lot of pain," he mutters, talking mostly to himself. "She's more dead than alive."

"Maybe it's not too late," Helena says from behind.

"Maybe not," Tim says, adding in his mind: *But I think it is.*

It's not just the woman's bad state that's making him pessimistic about his chances of healing her; it's also the fact that he now understands a bit more about how he does it. With both Helena and Buddy, he tapped into his love for them. He felt a deep connection to them. This woman, she's a stranger to him.

Only, that's not true. Not exactly.

Looking at her face, Tim can tell he's seen her before. It was a brief encounter, but he's always been good with faces.

I met her in the forest, he thinks. *Right before I found the boulder.*

He has no idea why the woman came to the cabin, but he understands how she found them: Having seen him walk around in the forest still wearing his pajama pants, she must have known Tim lived up here somewhere.

Did she come to help him? To protect him? Clearly, she's gone through a lot to get here. She should have gone to the hospital a long time ago, but evidently, it had been more important to her reaching him.

Tim takes a deep breath. "I think I'm ready," he tells himself. "Could you please turn down the music, honey?"

"What music?" Helena answers him from far away.

"That song," Tim mutters, closing his eyes. "I hate Clapton."

"Dad, what are you talking about?" His daughter's voice is tuning out. "There's no music playing. I think you ..."

Then, Tim is somewhere else.

42

VERONICA

SHE'S HUMMING A TUNE while lacing up her runners. Veronica hasn't felt this good in a long time. Her legs are ready, her muscles amped up, her mind excited for what's to come. The sun is shining outside. It's shaping up to become a perfect, warm spring day. She doesn't have a care in the world, and she's about to engage in her favorite activity.

Something else is making her happy this morning.

She did it.

She saved someone.

And not just someone. She saved *him*.

She's not sure who he is, but she knows he's important, and that's enough for her.

Veronica can't help but smile as she plugs in the AirPods. Before turning on the music, she pops her head into the bedroom. The curtains are drawn; Leo is still curled up below the covers. "See you later, babe," she tells him. He doesn't answer. He's probably sleeping. So she goes to the bed to kiss him goodbye … but as she pulls the blanket aside, she finds the bed empty.

Her smile falters for a moment.

"Oh," she mutters. "That's right. Leo's no longer here."

Did they break up?

Veronica isn't sure. Seeing Leo's side of the bed empty makes her a little sad. She doesn't want to feel sadness, though. Not today. It's a way too familiar feeling. A feeling she's been carrying around like a constant companion lately. But now she finally has the choice of putting it aside.

Going back out to the front door, she grabs her phone from the dresser to turn on the music. She sees a text. It's from Molly. Veronica's smile returns as she reads it.

Hey, Nica. Just wanted to say it was nice seeing you one last time at the cabin :) And please don't feel guilty. You did everything you could <3 M.

Reading Molly's text makes Veronica feel sad again. Even more so than before. She's still not sure why, but she suddenly gets the sense that something bad happened. It's almost like Molly is saying goodbye.

Veronica decides to text her back, so she writes: *Is everything okay, sweetie?*

As she sends it, a message pops up immediately: "The contact no longer exists."

Veronica frowns. She feels a heaviness settle over her heart. What happened to Molly? And Leo? Why is she feeling depressed when she thinks about them? It's a beautiful day outside, and she shouldn't be worried about a thing.

She decides not to investigate further. Whatever is going on, she probably can't do anything about it now anyway. She'll go for her run. That almost makes her feel better. Then, once she returns, she can deal with whatever is coming.

She turns on the music. The first song is *Wonderful Tonight*. It gives Veronica pause. She never put that song on her playlist. She's not really into ballads. They're too nostalgic for her taste, especially when she's running. But she decides to let it run.

Opening the door, Veronica jolts at the sight of the guy standing on the landing. "Jeez," she exclaims, taking out one of the AirPods. "Who are you?"

She knows who he is, of course. It's the guy from the woods. He's a little older than her, and considerably more worn. But his eyes are very much spirited. Fierce, even. Yet at the same time, friendly. Concerned.

"You shouldn't go," he tells her.

"Why not? I love running."

He shakes his head slowly. "If you leave now, you won't come back."

Veronica frowns. "What do you mean?" Clapton is singing about how wonderful his girl looks tonight.

The big guy extends his hand. "Come with me. You saved my life. Let me save yours."

"Save my life?" Veronica snorts. "What are you talking about? I'm not in any danger …"

He eyes her intently. "Look, this is your call. But I really think you should stick around."

"Why?" Veronica asks again. For some odd reason, her voice breaks. "There's nothing left for me. They're all gone. And it's my fault. Besides …" She scoffs. "I'm dead already. See?" Without thinking, she lifts up her shirt to show him the tiny scars. "Six months, tops."

His eyes go from the scars and back up to her face. "A lot can happen in six months. You could do a lot of good, you know. To the world."

Veronica smiles, and as she does, a big, warm tear rolls down her cheek. "I think I already saved the world. Or at least I gave it a fighting chance."

He nods slowly. "You did."

Veronica swallows, forcing the smile to stay on. "You've got a daughter, right?"

"I do."

"Hug her from me."

"If you come with me, you can hug her yourself."

"No," Veronica says, still smiling. She closes her eyes for a moment and takes a deep breath. "No, I'm done."

Opening her eyes again, the guy is still looking at her. "Are you sure?"

"Absolutely. I'm going for that run now."

She doesn't move; she waits for him to get out of her way. And he does. Taking a step sideways, he doesn't take his eyes off of hers. "Okay, then."

"Okay, then," Veronica says.

She halfway expects him to grab her. And he does extend his hand again, but as an invitation. She takes it squeezes it briefly.

"Thank you," he says.

"You're welcome," she says.

Then she puts the AirPod back in and heads down the stairs. The song is still going, growing louder in her ears, telling her it's time to go home now, and Veronica's smile returns as she ups the speed. She can't wait to get out there. To do what she loves.

As she descends the stairs two steps at a time, she thinks again about Leo and Molly and even Alice and Flemming and Sylvia, and this time, the sadness in her heart turns into something else, something much lighter, and she suddenly understands that they're all waiting for her out there, and Veronica feels like her heart is about to burst from joy as she runs down the stairs even faster.

43

HELENA

SHE'S SLUMPED OVER IN the armchair, a blanket wrapped around herself, the warmth from the fire slowly heating up the room. Her right arm is hanging over the side, her hand caressing the top of Buddy's head. The dog is lying on the floor, breathing deeply.

Helena is fighting to stay awake. It's been an incredibly long day, and she's exhausted beyond belief.

Still, she wants to stay alert in case her dad needs her.

He's been sitting in the same position for twenty minutes now. His eyes closed, his forehead slightly wrinkled, his hand resting on the woman's thigh. He hasn't moved, hasn't made a sound.

The woman, on the other hand, shifts now and then, groans or mutters in her sleep. She's not waking up, and her breathing becomes more and more shallow.

Suddenly, Helena sits up with a grunt, feeling a string of saliva at the corner of her mouth. She wipes it away, realizing she'd drifted off despite herself.

Her dad's eyes are open, looking at the woman. He's removed his hand from her leg. The woman is still just lying there. She's calmer now, but she's still not awake.

"Dad?" Helena says, clearing her throat. "Did it ... did it work?"

He answers her only with a single, deep breath.

Buddy gets up and slinks to the woman. He licks her cheek once, then comes back over to Helena. Looking closer at the woman's face, Helena notices how she looks slightly different. Her face has shrunk a little, her mouth open just a crack. She's no longer breathing.

"She's ... she's dead," Helena hears herself say. It's weird. She didn't know the woman—she's never even met her—and yet she feels a deep sadness at her dying.

Her dad runs a hand through his hair, then gets to his feet.

"You couldn't save her?" Helena asks, looking up at him.

"Wasn't my call," he says simply, then turns and walks to the kitchen.

For a moment, Helena is struck by a strong déjà-vu at how her dad is acting. It's exactly how he'd always get whenever she or her mom was trying to get him to talk about anything important. He'd clam up, shut down, walk away. She starts to feel upset, angry even. She wants to say something. Ask him to elaborate. Demand that he doesn't regress and resort to his old ways of doing things now that they're finally starting to find each other.

But she holds back the urge to speak. Instead, she sits with her frustration for a moment. Feeling it burn in her throat.

She hears her dad drink greedily and loudly from the tap in the kitchen, and it makes her even more annoyed that he's more concerned about quenching his thirst than answering her questions or honoring the woman who just saved all their lives.

Still, she doesn't say anything. She really wants to play her part in fixing their relationship, and as distressed as she's feeling right now, something tells her the mature thing to do is not to start blaming him but give him space. She's seen her mom do it tons of times. Helena never got it and always felt her mom should've pressed the point instead of just letting it go. But maybe ... just maybe, there was wisdom in keeping quiet.

Her dad comes back to the living room. He stops in front of the couch and looks down at the woman. "Her name was Veronica."

Helena blinks. "Did you know her?"

"No. I've seen her once. It was very brief. We never spoke."

More silence.

Helena swallows. "We should ... we should tell her family."

"They're all gone," he says bluntly.

"Oh."

Suddenly, it dawns on Helena that her dad isn't being glib because he finds the situation uncomfortable. He's doing it out of respect for the woman.

"What ... what should we do, then?"

"I'm going to bury her." He turns to look at her, and to her surprise, she sees a tear at the corner of his eye. Despite the half-faded pupil, he looks more human than she's probably ever seen him. She instinctively gets up and goes to him, and he takes her into a tight hug.

"Don't feel bad," she says quietly. "You did what you could."

Her dad takes a shaky breath, then he says, "When I'm done, we should leave. It's not safe here."

She looks up at him and sees determination coming back over his face. "Because of the hatch? I'm sorry, Dad. I couldn't help it. The alien, it just destroyed it ..."

"I know. It would've happened anyway. They know about this place. I'm sure it's just a matter of time before more of them show up."

Helena frowns. "You told me they knew about me because of Alan. He knew I work at BESTSELLER. Did he also know about this place?"

"I don't think he did. He always billed me at the fake address. I don't know, maybe they have some other way of finding me. It doesn't really matter right now."

Helena nods in the direction of the driveway. "Did you know the person out there?"

"I think I know who he was. I think I heard his voice once. He said something about feeling powerful. Then I forgot about him. It was a mistake." He takes another deep breath and looks around the living room. "So many memories. I thought I was gonna live out my days here."

She knows he's referring to her mom. She understands that leaving this would be like losing even more of her. She wants to say something to give him hope. "Maybe we'll return one day. When this is all over."

He looks down at her, his expression one of surprise. "You think there's a happy ending?"

Another strong sense of déjà-vu, this one so forceful that for a split second, it sends her back in time to the hospital room her mom died in.

"*I'm really scared, Mom*," Helena had said, choked by tears. "*What if this doesn't end well?*"

Her mother had smiled at her for the last time and told her—

"There's always a happy ending, Dad. It's just a matter of how much you need to go through first."

He searches her face, as though sensing the words are coming from somewhere else. Then he smiles and says, "I hope you're right."

His expression turns serious again, and they're quiet for another moment.

Helena can't help but ask, "So ... where do we go now, Dad?"

"Honestly, I don't know." He turns towards the window facing the forest. "But before we go anywhere, I need to head back over there. It's calling me." That last part he mutters under his breath, almost like he's talking to himself.

Helena doesn't like the thought of him venturing into the woods alone to go find that evil thing that started everything. "Are you sure that's a good idea? What if it's dangerous?"

"It can't do anything to me that it hasn't tried already."

"But ... couldn't it be a trap? If they know what you know, then maybe there's, like, twenty of them waiting out there?"

Her dad is quiet for a few seconds. Buddy gives off a low whimper, as though he also doesn't care for the idea.

Finally, her dad says, "It could be a trap. But there's something else out there, too. Something they don't want me to know." He looks at her, and his pupils are unusually visible, shining with that old stubbornness she knows so well. "That's why I gotta do it."

***

If you want to learn how things began, you should check out the free prequel, *Blackout*.
It's only available at **nick-clausen.com/blackout**

Or, if you want to continue onwards, you can grab Book 3 at
nick-clausen.com/invaders3

Printed in Dunstable, United Kingdom